RYKER

Owatonna U Hockey, 1

_____

RJ SCOTT
V.L. LOCEY

Love Lane Books

Ryker (Owatonna U #1)

Copyright © 2018 RJ Scott, Copyright © 2018 V.L. Locey

Cover design by Meredith Russell, Edited by Sue Laybourn

Published by Love Lane Books Limited

ISBN: 9781785645501

All Rights Reserved

RYKER

OWATONNA U HOCKEY#1

RJ SCOTT & V.L. LOCEY

Love Lane Books

Prologue

THE COMMENTATOR WAS AGITATED. "IT LOOKS LIKE WE HAVE a Railer down… it's Tennant Rowe. I can confirm that Tennant Rowe is on the ice. Is he moving? It doesn't look as if he's moving."

There was so much blood. When the teams backed away, all I could see was Ten splayed on the ice as if his strings had been cut.

"Tennant Rowe isn't moving. This looks bad. The paramedics are with him."

The door to my room flew open, Mom standing there, white as a sheet. "Ryker." She looked from me to the television.

"I need to go to…"

"Ian will take you where you need to go, grab some stuff. He's getting the car out now."

I was crying, I think, and I felt sick. So fucking sick.

All I knew was that I had to get to Dad, needed to be there for him.

And for Ten.

ONE

Ryker

AS MUCH AS TENNANT ROWE, HOCKEY PHENOM AND FACE OF the Railers franchise, tried, there was no way he was going to go undetected attending this year's NHL draft as one of my family.

I knew that. Dad knew that.

Ten, on the other hand, was convinced that a ball cap pulled low over his face would be enough to stop anyone from knowing he was in the building.

The place filled with hundreds of potential hockey draftees, their hockey-loving parents, siblings, coaches, and managers of all the NHL teams, camera crews, and anyone else who'd managed to get a seat in the vast auditorium.

"It's not going to work," I said, tugging the bill of the cap lower over Ten's forehead.

"I just won't look anyone in the eye." Ten used a single finger to push the cap back up again.

Dad thrust his cell phone in front of Ten and wiggled it a little.

"I can't read it if you keep moving it," Ten muttered, and held Dad's hand still.

Dad huffed and read it out. "Ten-Watch have one hundred and ten thousand 'yes' votes on a poll of whether you'll be here to support your, and I quote, sexy husband and his adorable son."

I couldn't help the snigger that escaped me at that point. Ten-Watch was a fanatical group of Railers' hockey fans who had decided Ten was edible, and yes, those were the words they used. Dad and I figured on the account as well. Jared Madsen, a former hard man of the NHL, had been labeled as the sexy husband. I was the adorable son, and it never failed to make me smile, given there were only a few years between Ten and me. I quite liked being called adorable as long as people remembered I was also a hockey player, but Dad found the whole sexy-husband-of-an-NHL-star discomforting.

Ten leaned into Dad and kissed him, then patted his cheek. "You are sexy," he pointed out.

Which led to Dad huffing and then kissing him back. I loved the small shows of affection I saw between them. Mom and Dad had divorced some time back, and even though she was happily married to Ian, the stockbroker, and they had three kids (all girls) together, I'd always worried Dad would stay alone.

Then he'd met Ten, and they were ridiculously good together. I always got the warm and fuzzies when they were so comfortable, laughing and kissing, and just being in love. One day I would have that as well.

One day, I would meet the perfect person. After hockey, of course. I had an entire NHL career spread out in front of me, and I was going to put everything I had into that. Romance could wait awhile.

"Ready to do this, son?" Dad took one last shot at straightening my tie.

I let him fix it. This was his day as well, and I'd already had Mom straightening the tie before she'd left to find her seat, along with Ian and my half-sisters, Sophia, Ava and Lilly.

"Ready as I'll ever be," I reassured him and pushed back my shoulders. I wasn't a star as Ten had been at his draft. I wasn't first-round pick material, but I was an excellent two-hundred-foot skater, with skills, and three generations of hockey experience behind me. I had a future, and I felt it in my bones that I would be picked by a team today. This is what every young hockey player dreams of, to be picked by a national team and being nurtured by them so that a man could do precisely what he wanted to do with his life.

"Your grandpa is all serious and proud today," Dad warned me.

"It's fine; we're good," I reassured him and smiled to underline just how happy I was that my family was there. Even if one of them was my grandpa, whom I called GP, and who wanted me to go straight into playing at national level, even if I knew I wasn't ready just yet. I could deal with GP and had no qualms about telling him exactly how I felt. He'd also straightened my tie, which seemed to be a thing, then hugged me and told me to do well.

He expected me to do well, always had. Only he was convinced his way, of playing professionally at a young age, was the only route to making a career for myself. Dad, on the other hand, told me I had choices and helped me see that college hockey for a few years was a good option.

"Okay, we're making our way down." Dad patted my arm. "You have ten minutes, okay?"

The door flew open and startled us all, but I relaxed when I saw Andy Foster, fellow player and potential draft pick, also a friend from college, possibly the only one I really had. His grin turned to an expression of awe when he realized he'd burst in on family time, and then it transformed into an adoring stare as he realized Tennant Rowe was in the room. I'd seen it happen before, and one day, I am sure one of my hockey friends would actually bow in front of Ten.

"God, I'm a huge fan," he said to Ten and held out a hand to shake.

Ten was gracious, friendly, and then tugged down the hat again.

I snorted another laugh and cuffed Andy around the head as Ten and Jared left.

"He's just another guy," I said, dodging Andy's retaliation as he went to muss my hair. "Hey, no one touches the hair."

I checked in the mirror one last time. If I got picked today, no, not if, when, then the photo they took of me in my new team's jersey would be one I kept forever. I needed to look good.

I was cursed with my mom's curls, but the compromise was having to get it cut and styled every four weeks so it appeared controlled, even after I'd been wearing a helmet. I'd shaved without managing to cut myself, messed with my hair using a ton of product. There was nothing else to do.

"What's your seat number?"

I picked up my pass. "D47."

Andy waved his in front of my nose. "E46, right behind you."

We headed for the arena, and even though I'd seen the draft on television every year since I was old enough to know what it was, I stopped in awe when I entered the main hall. Where there usually was ice, there was a sea of tables, each one occupied by an NHL team, thirty-two of them, and huddled around the tables were general managers, coaches, owners, all frantically passing notes between each other. I spotted the owner of Boston conversing with the head coach of the Dragons, deep in discussion, probably deciding the fate of a draft pick today.. I wondered if it was me they were talking about. I'd be cool with either of those teams, staying up in the Northeast.

Of course, it wasn't about me. They would be wheeling and dealing about one of the new generational talents, no doubt.

I took my seat and bumped elbows with Dad, glancing around him at Ten who was slumped, unsuccessfully hiding in his seat. Then I turned the other way to Mom and Ian, and saw my sisters chattering excitedly. That enthusiasm would probably wane after a while; the draft was a long process, and as they were aged between six and nine, the likelihood of them getting bored was quite high, despite the iPads they had on their knees. Grandpa was here as well, and he nodded at me. That was pretty much all I was going to get from him.

The noise died, signaling the start of it all, and our attention turned to the podium. This year's draft had begun.

I only began to panic when it neared the end of the first round. Each team got to pick an up-and-coming player on each round unless they'd traded away that right for some reason, and I hadn't been picked up yet. Dad had said I was first-round material, but what if he was wrong?

Next up were the Arizona Raptors, who were not on the list of teams I wanted to play for. I had a feeling for who I thought would be the best fit, and the Raptors had a reputation that made me feel a hundred kinds of uncomfortable. They were the dark team of the NHL, the ones with the most fights, the dirty hits, and players with bad reputations. This was where the hard guys played, with their shady moves and constantly getting up in other players faces. I wanted a team that played hockey with skill and speed. Maybe I would go top of the second round. That wouldn't be so bad.

The manager of the Raptors, a short, rotund guy with thinning hair, went up to the podium, and the arena hushed as it had done every time. He waffled a little about how honored he was to be here, thanked Vancouver for hosting, talked about its hockey heritage, and how beautiful the city was, and then he cleared his throat.

"The Arizona Raptors are proud to select, from Leicester college…"

My heart sank. There was only Andy and me there from Leicester, and the word was the Raptors were looking for wingers, not D-men like Andy. Shit. Shit. Shit. I didn't know whether to be afraid or ecstatic.

Dad tensed next to me. "It will be okay," he murmured, just for me to hear.

"…Ryker Madsen!" the manager finished.

Everyone in my group cheered. I stood, and Dad hugged me, Mom was crying and kissing my hair, GP smiled broadly, his chest puffed out with pride, and Ten whooped, throwing his hat in the hair, caution be damned. Sophia, Ava and Lilly stood on their chairs, and then Ava jumped onto me and clung to me like a monkey, squealing loudly.

Mom peeled her off with Ian's help. Then I had to leave them all abruptly and do the next bit on my own.

I'd been drafted. First round. Pick twenty-six out of the hundreds of guys my age.

Drafted to the Arizona Raptors.

My stomach felt a little touchy, and my palms were damp, but my excitement overtook any immediate worries I had, and I headed to the stage, shaking hands, pulling on the brown-and-gold jersey of the Raptors, and posing for the photograph.

"Good things," the manager was saying, pumping my hand and grinning widely. "I see good things for you. We're building a franchise… high hopes… development… college… three-year plan…" he repeated the same things as I stood dumb, listening.

I couldn't hear everything he was saying, but I gave the answer he expected. "I'm excited for the chance," I said back.

And I was.

I mean, I really *was* excited. An NHL team had chosen me. I would be at college, developing my skills, working hard, and in three years, I would be out on the ice as part of the Raptors. Unless they wanted me sooner, of course.

I might fuck up somewhere or get injured or not make the cut, but none of that was worth worrying about right now.

Maybe the Raptors would want me straight away. I had completed my first year of college, and I'd promised Dad I'd give it another year, but when all you want to do is play hockey, then learning algebra or writing essays on Shakespeare or studying for exams was pointless. Maybe I'd join the Raptors earlier. Who needed college anyway?

I was the captain of my own destiny, and right now, in this arena, I was invincible.

ANDY WAS TAKEN in the third round, by the Boston team, and Ten had a lot to say about that. In fact, he had something to say about every draft pick: detailed summaries, pros, cons, the kind of game they played. He lived and breathed hockey, which is what made him one of the best.

Thing was, even when we were at dinner, celebrating the

draft and the fact I'd been picked, he still hadn't summarized me.

He was sitting next to me, chatting at length with the youngest of my sisters, Lilly, explaining how birds flew or something that sounded like it. I doubted it was scientifically correct when I heard the word magic, but Lilly was transfixed. Only when he'd finished did I nudge him with my elbow. He side-eyed me and nudged me back. We had that kind of friendship, one that drove my Dad mad at times.

"How would you sum me up?" I asked him outright.

He blinked at me, then looked me up and down while chewing on a fry.

"Too skinny, and you leave your towels on the floor."

I shoved him, and he made an exaggerated fall backward, scooping a squealing Lilly with him as he went. Dad got involved then, asking what the hell was going on, with a long-suffering sigh.

"The kids are at it again," he murmured, and Ten started laughing, infectiously.

When Ten stopped laughing, he grew more serious, turned to me and grasped my shoulders.

"Graceful, imaginative, an explosive skater with breakaway speed, who will go faster with conditioning and training. You have balance and the ability to control the puck at high speeds, and that's only matched by a few others at your pick level in this draft. You're extremely shifty, and sometimes you get too arrogant and don't pass, but you can change gears effortlessly, especially to the outside. Skills for chipping and retrieving the puck into an open area, then turning it into a high-quality scoring chance are good. You make hard, crisp passes on both forehand and backhand, and at times you can be tough to contain and seal off. You show frustration when things don't go your way, but you don't lose your temper. You have hockey smarts, and with time, Ryker Madsen, I would be honored to have you playing on my wing."

Tears pricked my eyes, and I swallowed because I wasn't going to damn well cry in front of a tableful of my family.

GP made a noise of disagreement, and I heard him start to explain how Ten was wrong. I didn't need to know what I was bad at, because I was ready for the big leagues. I also heard Dad and Mom both hush him.

Ten peered at me. "Shit, did I make you cry?"

I punched him. "Obviously not, asshole," I muttered and then covered my emotion by eating my pasta.

But we elbowed each other, and it didn't matter that I didn't have too many friends at college or that I was seen as some weird, freaky way to get to Ten or the Railers.

I had my Mom, always in my corner. My Dad, fiercely protective and a cool dude. My sisters who made my life brighter and who would, under no circumstances, ever date a hockey player. And I had Ten in my corner, and he had faith in my skills. Even my grandpa was proud of me, and I could handle his interference most of the time.

Mostly I had family who cared about me.; I was blessed and the luckiest guy alive.

And I also had hockey.

WHEN WE GOT HOME, Dad parked his Land Rover next to a shiny silver Mercedes. Not a new car. It had been decorated with a huge red ribbon and a sign that said, *Congratulations, Ryker*. I could see the brand-new sticks and skates arranged on the hood, along with a whole pile of Railers' stuff. Talk about the perfect end to a perfect day!

Dad handed me the key.

"The car is from me and your mom. Ten added all the other stuff. That should set you up," he said a little gruffly.

We got out of his car, and he hugged me.

"I love you, Dad, thank you."

"I love you too, Ry. Be happy, okay?"

Yep, I was blessed.

TWO

Jacob

"JACOB?"

Mom's voice slipped into my sleep, nudging the remnants of a familiar fantasy aside. The dream faded quickly as light crept into my world, but the feeling of kicking off fetters lingered for another second or two.

"Jacob, come on now. You have to get up." She shook me gently, her voice kind yet firm, the aroma of fried bacon clinging to her.

"I'm up." I wasn't fully, but it wouldn't have been the first time I'd staggered into the milking parlor half-asleep. I'd done it all through high school. "I slept through my alarm."

"He's been down there for over a half hour."

I blinked at my mother, her face firmly set, her gaze filled with apprehension. She knew my father as well as anyone, certainly as well as I did. He had never raised a hand to me for my many infractions over the years, but his verbal assaults were brutal.

"Come on and get some clothes on before he comes back to the house looking for you. You know he hates that."

"Right, yep, I'm up." I threw aside the thin covering, sat

up, and scrubbed my face with my hands. "Can you have a slice of toast ready for me?"

"Of course." She ruffled my hair, then left me to get dressed. There was no time wasted stepping into yesterday's jeans and yanking them over my briefs. I found a dirty T-shirt in the hamper, tugged that over my head, and thundered down the stairs of our old farmhouse. My mother waited at the front door with a slice of toast with butter and jam.

"Thanks, Mom." I grabbed the slice of toast, kissed her cheek, and shoved my feet into my sneakers, pushing out into the soft grayish-pink dawn. The lowing of the Holsteins waiting to be let into the milking parlor greeted me, as did the first call of a bird. I chewed and ran, getting the toast eaten as I passed two silos on my way to the barn. The closer I got, the louder the cows became, calling out to me to let me know just how full their udders were.

I burst into the mudroom, kicked off my sneakers, stepping into green knee-high rubber boots after I pulled on some genuinely hideous high-vis yellow rubber overalls, all covered with cow shit. My first roommate at Owatonna had mentioned that I carried the smell with me whenever I came back from a trip home. When you're a farmer, you develop a blind nose to the smell because there is just no escaping it. Farming is a dirty, hard job.

I dashed past the room that housed the two 500-gallon bulk tanks that held all the milk we gathered on a daily basis and burst into the milking parlor, my father's unhappy gaze landing on me immediately. He was a tall man, fit, brown haired, blue eyed, stubborn, and well worn by life, like most farmers. We lived pretty much from milk check to milk check. Mom always said I was a Benson through and through, right down to the way I cocked my chin when I was bullish.

"Sorry I'm late," I yelled over the loud pulsing sound of the milking machines. "I slept through the alarm."

"If you used a real alarm clock instead of that damn cell phone, you'd be able to get up and tend to your chores on time." *And good morning to you too, Dad. For fuck sake.* "Get those cows off the line."

"Yep. On it." And so the drudgery of a day on a dairy farm began. As much as I loved this life, I hated it just as much. That made no sense. I knew that, but there it was. I'd grown up on this three-hundred-acre farm. It was home, and I loved the land, the animals, and the history of our homestead. This place had been in our family for five generations. It would probably die with me, since my chances of breeding another Benson were nil. It was up to me—the only Benson to ever go to college—to find a way to save this operation for the next generation who would never be. Talk about some irony.

There was little conversation between my father and me as we moved the hundred and fifty head through the milking parlor. Even as the last group, mostly first-year heifers who were still new to the milking routine, were herded in, Dad and I said nothing. There was no need, really. I knew what to do, what was expected of me, and how much was riding on me. I also was aware of how disappointed he was in me for being gay and killing off the proud tradition of Benson dairy farmers by my lack of interest in knocking up my future wife repeatedly.

As if my liking boys would do that by itself. More than likely, the vast corporate farms and low milk prices would be what finally killed the small, independent farmer. Unless I could use my degree in ag science to find a way to save us.

No pressure, Jacob. Just do something to make them proud, for once.

"You need to dip those teats," Dad shouted down the line to me.

"I know, Dad." He threw me a look that told me he was not amused by my curt reply. "I've been doing this since I was eight. I know what you want from me." I just wasn't sure I could deliver.

"Then stop staring off into space. Bad enough you're leaving me here alone to run off to that damn hockey camp."

And here we went. Dad began the tired litany of this camp, hockey, the cost, the time away from the farm, the haying that he would have to hire help for, the milking that my mother would have to help with, the cost, the cost, the cost, and the fucking cost. He had no idea how vital ice hockey was to me. I mean, he understood that my hockey scholarship paid for me to study ag science, which would, we all hoped, pull us from the brink of foreclosure. He just disliked how much time I had to spend on the sport that would cover my college costs.

"…not even drafted. You're never going to be able to make a living with the damn sport, so why are we shelling out money for this fancy camp all the way in Ontario when you could be here doing the work that needs to be done?"

I walked out of the parlor, patting the last heifer on the ass, leaving him talking to himself. Yeah, he was right, the cost of this summer conditioning camp was steep, but I'd saved up for more than half of the high-performance course. Three grand was steep, and I knew that coughing up half of the fee had dipped into my parents' bank account deeply, but the entire OU Eagles team was attending this camp. As my father liked to point out, I wasn't the best hockey player on the team, which was why I had to participate in this camp. I had to keep pace with the rest of the team, or I'd be cut. And if I were cut, there went my money and the degree and all that hope my family had piled onto my back. Also, I just loved hockey. It might not have been my life calling, and I knew that I'd never be a Tennant Rowe, but when I was out on the ice, all this pressure was gone. It was me, the ice, the puck, and the game. It was my one escape from a life that weighed on me more and more heavily with each passing day.

"Get moving," I barked, clapping an older cow on her bony ass, moving the herd into the lounging area where they'd spend the day eating, drinking, sleeping, chewing their cuds, and making more milk for the evening milking. "Go on! Hyah! Move, cow."

The cows shuffled along, content to mosey now that their bags were empty. I paused at the metal gate as a few old gals ambled past, and looked out over our land. The acres of hay were now pink with the rising sun. Crows flew overhead, cawing at each other, heading to the cornfields possibly or just circling around the barn as dawn gilded the steel roof of our milk barn rosy pink and salmon. This was the part of farming that I adored. These moments out on the land, the gentle swish of tails and the soft moo of cattle, the buzz of flies warming to the day, the smell of freshly cut hay, and the sight of the Benson house nestled among towering oaks that my great-great-grandfather had planted. Nothing was more beautiful than Minnesota farmland.

A certain bovine nudged me in the back, pushing me into the gate. I chuckled and reached back to find Matilda, one of the last cows I had taken to the Eden Crossing county fair. She was six now and still as affectionate as she had been when she'd been a young heifer and had won me several blue ribbons. I missed those days: running wild for a week on the fairgrounds, sleeping in the dairy barn with the other 4-H and FFA kids, kissing Dirk Manning under the bleachers during the country classics concert. Back then, life was just cows, school, hockey, and discovering how much I liked cute boys, like Dirk. Before my sexuality had become an issue with my community and my farming groups, before college and the killer pressure that had brought, before I had been forced to come out to our small, conservative town.

I stood to the side to allow the big black-and-white Holstein to stand next to me. I ran a hand over her head, scratching between her ears. She always did enjoy scratches. We stood there for several minutes, the dawdlers finally making their way to the fenced-in area where they'd loaf for the day. Matilda stayed with me until the roar of the milk truck rattling down the long, dusty lane broke into the morning calm.

"Jacob!" His voice blasted out of the barn. "Still work to be done, boy!"

"Coming!" I shouted back at my father, pushed Matilda along, shut the gate, and then slugged my way back to the barn, secretly willing the next two hours to hurry by so I could get on the road. I loved this farm, but sometimes it felt like it was killing me, one disapproving or disappointed look at a time.

THE THIRTEEN-HOUR-PLUS DRIVE to Plover Lake, Ontario, was made even longer because I had to stop every two hours to add oil to my old Ford pickup. She leaked. A lot. But there were no funds in the bank to buy me a new vehicle, so I made do with the old workhorse Ford that one of my cousins had sold me for a hundred bucks when I'd turned sixteen. Personally, I think I paid ninety-nine dollars too much, but so goes it for poor farm boys.

After close to fifteen hours behind the wheel, I was stiff, crabby, hungry, and tired. I passed through the small town of

Plover Lake just the other side of eight p.m. All the stores on Main were closed, aside from a bar. The tiny little hamlet reminded me of Eden Crossing in so many ways. The major difference was that red-and-white flags with maple leaves hung outside of every shop.

The Rayzor Edge Performance & Wellness Center sat on fifty acres of Canadian wilderness at the base of Blue Mountain. Plover Lake rested next to the massive facility, which included an NHL-sized rink that was attached to the main wellness center. Pulling around back, I found the dorm buildings where the players were housed. The night was just tickling the clear blue sky, darkening the edges of a long day, when I parked in front of the long brick dorms. I'd been assigned to the red dorm which was marked with a big X on the map I'd been sent. Registration took forever, or maybe it just seemed that way because I was exhausted.

After taking the elevator to the second floor, I hauled my ass, my gear, and my bags to room 211 and swiped my scarlet key card. The room was big, airy, and had a great view of Plover Lake. I claimed the bed by the window because I was there earlier and that gave me first dibs. As soon as I got hooked into the free Wi-Fi, I texted my mother to let her know that I'd arrived safely. She called back shortly after the text as I was trying to decide where to put the books for my summer course in Farm Management and Operations. I stacked them on a desk by the window, tossed down my laptop and a couple of notebooks, and spent a few minutes talking with Mom as I put my stuff away. After the fourth yawn in her ear, she sent me to bed, passing along love from her and Dad.

My stomach rumbled, but I was too done in to feed it. Stripping down to my underwear, I then turned off the light on the nightstand between the double beds and fell instantly asleep.

MORNING LIGHT FELL on my face. I lay there for several minutes, breathing in the knowledge that I didn't have to face my father in the dairy barn today. I could feel the pound of stress lift from my shoulders. Hunger spurred me to get up. After using the toilet and taking a fast shower, I grabbed my textbook for Farm Management and Operations. If I could complete this course during the summer, I could add Working with Animals in the fall. That course dealt on hands-on husbandry skills which was my favorite activity of being part of the agriculture business.

The crinkled map in hand, I stepped outside, inhaled the fresh air, and watched in mild fascination as a 550 horsepower Range Rover pulled up. I'd never seen one in person, although I had a photo of one on my pin board at home. Not one person in Eden Crossing could afford such an ostentatious car. It was a beauty; deep red, sleek, and shiny. A book under my arm, I waited, knowing that whoever climbed out of it would be upper crust, clad in the best clothes and carrying the best gear. And yeah, I was right. Top-of-the-line stick, pricey skates, brand-new pads. I hadn't pictured the rich boy being so hot, but looks don't mean a thing when you're an uppity snob. Mr. Money Jr. was tall, firm, long-legged, and possessed some of the thickest, darkest hair I had ever seen. I rubbed my hand over my short hair and frowned. My mother cut my hair because why pay fifteen bucks to the barber? This guy probably spent a hundred bucks to get his hair styled.

He spun around, looking a little lost, talking the whole while with a big blond man whom I instantly recognized as

Jared Madsen. I would have pegged him as a defenseman just from his bulk and carriage. Old-school D-men all had that look. It's hard to describe it exactly, but they were burly bastards who knew how tough they were, and that confidence oozed out of them. So, if that was Jared Madsen, Richie Rich there had to be his son, Ryker. I'd seen a few fuzzy images of the three of them—Jared, Ryker and Tennant—online at some rock concert they'd flown to. Talk about a charmed life. The only concert I'd ever attended had been some washed-out country singer at the Eden Crossing fair.

Ryker turned to face the cool wind coming down the mountain. The rowdy air lifted all that hair of his. It was long and lush. I bet he had great flow. It probably felt like satin between a man's fingers…

Knowing I had seen enough of the cash-and-flash, I headed toward the central facility, found the dining hall and the rest of the Eagles, and sat down to fill up on fresh fruit, whole wheat toast with jam, oatmeal, and milk. My teammates all called out as I passed, the only one jumping up with his tray and following me to a corner table was Benoit Morin, one of two Eagles goalies. Ben, as we called him, was an upbeat Quebecer who smiled a great deal, told the corniest jokes, listened to a lot of Frank Ocean and Drake, and worshipped Malcolm Subban. We'd hit it off first thing, and he was probably the closest friend I had on the team.

"Thanks for dropping me a note letting me know you were here," Ben said, then popped a chunk of melon into his mouth. I gave the lanky black man a tired glance and flipped open my book. He reached over, fingers coated with fruit juice, and closed the textbook. "Nope, man, no way. Not today. Study time is later. Daytime here is all about the hockey."

"Got to cram it in when I can," I reminded him.

Ben rolled his eyes, about to say something about giving myself a break or cutting back on the books or going out on a date. Ben was big on being social. When you looked like him, social was easy. He was one beautiful man. A man who looked like me—big and homespun with a common sort of face—who carried the smell of a barn with him, being a social butterfly wasn't quite in the cards. He opened his mouth to say something when a disturbance at the cafeteria door grabbed our attention.

"No shit, you know who that is?" Ben waved his slice of pineapple at Mr. Rich Boy and a pudgy man in a red staff polo coming through the door. "That's Ryker Madsen."

"Yeah, I know."

"And you're not impressed?"

"Not really, no."

He wasn't wrong. I mean, I couldn't get my head out of the books, but equally, I needed to pay more attention to the guys around me in the hockey community.

Ben shoved a fat red grape into his mouth, chewed, and hurried to swallow while I stared at Mr. Wealth, the one with the pretty face and L'Oréal locks from the parking lot. "Ryker Madsen is the son of Jared Madsen, the defensive coach of the Railers. His father is living with Tennant Rowe, a hockey god. And you're not the least bit impressed?"

"Not really. Ryker Madsen has probably had everything bought and paid for by his father. When he has to work to prove himself and earn his way, then I'll pay attention." I went back to my book.

"Wonder who he's rooming with. Man, if we could get in close with him, we could get to meet his father and Tennant Rowe. I'm going to go introduce myself."

"Knock yourself out. I don't bow and scrape for rich people."

"JB, come on, don't be so *you*."

When I looked at Ryker Madsen flashing straight white teeth and a small dimple as he was engulfed by my team, my resolve to keep my distance doubled. I refused to be a sycophant, sucking up to him because he had money and was close to a hockey god.

"Nope, not interested in his type." I'd seen the snide glances tossed my way by the elite on campus. Running over to kiss this rich kid's thousand-dollar sneakers? Thanks but no thanks.

"Fine. Be yourself then. Save me a place in line for the opening day tour." Ben shot to his feet, wiped his sticky fingers on his gym shorts, and joined the throng of admirers gathering around Ryker. Damn guys acted as if they'd never seen famous people before. I went back to my textbook, uninterested in the drooling taking place by the breakfast buffet tables. Hopefully, I'd be able to keep a wide berth from Mr. Ryker Madsen and his millions.

THREE

Ryker

I PULLED MY BAGS OUT OF THE CAR, HOISTED ONE OVER MY shoulder, balancing the other with sticks.

"I think that's everything," I couldn't close the trunk of the sexy red Range Rover, but Dad did it for me and then turned to me with a grin on his face.

"I love this place," he exclaimed, for what had to be the hundredth time since I'd agreed on the place I wanted to train in the summer. The Rayzor Edge Performance & Wellness Center sat on the shores of Plover Lake, and was renowned for its work with the newbies like me, recently drafted, staying at college, improving skills.

The Raptors said they wanted me better, faster, stronger. They wanted me to stay in college for the time being. That stung a little, but as Dad said, there were always options. Starting with this training school.

It was owned run by a friend of Dad's, Ethan Powell, a former teammate, and now a conditioning coach. The rink looked cool, the accommodation neat, but it was learning from Ethan that had me most excited.

Dad was thrilled when I'd said I would go, but it hadn't been a hard decision to make.

There would be a mix of players there, some draft picks like me, others a year behind, working for the draft, and some who just paid the extortionate fees to work on their game for four weeks. The cross-section of skaters was an exciting prospect, and I couldn't wait to meet everyone.

Andy was here. He'd been picked up by the Bears in the third round, and I hoped I was rooming with him just as I did at college. This was going to be an excellent summer, hockey, beer, parties, and best of all, a chance to decide what I was doing next.

"Can we talk, Dad," I began cautiously. I'd held off mentioning it on the drive there, instead focusing on the talk about the Railers and the new post-Stanley Cup season. Dad was still on a high, and Ten wouldn't stop talking about it at home. One day that would be me, holding the cup for real in my own right. I just had to keep my nose clean, work hard.

Yeah, one day it will be mine.

Dad pocketed his keys and looked at me expectantly. "
"Of course, what's up?"

"I'm not..." Jeez, how did I word this? Dad, I want to give up college because the hockey at Leicester is shit, and I hate it, and the coach is an asshole who is fucking with me because of who I am and who you are and the fact I know Ten, and I really want to leave.

"Are you okay, son?" Dad held my shoulders. I knew I could tell him anything. He was open-minded, supportive, loved me, wanted the best for my career, and I decided honesty was the best way to go.

"It's college. I don't want to be there."

He nodded and didn't immediately jump on me. College was

important to my Dad. He never went, but he wanted more for me, or at least that's what he said. I thought the life he had—coaching with the Railers, living with Ten, was all good, but who was I to judge. I guess parents always want the best for their kids.

"College in general? Or Leicester College specifically?"

How did I answer that? I just wanted to play hockey, that was all, but I also knew I needed the development time to grow into my body, to learn more, to become better. I wasn't stupid. I'd listened to what the Raptors manager had told me, even if what he spouted wasn't precisely being actioned in his team at the moment. I knew I was an excellent hockey player. More than that. I was what the Raptors needed.

Development camp had been a wake-up call. Along with nineteen returners from last year's camp, there were twenty-three new guys and also the six picks the Raptors had in the draft. I was one of forty-eight, and it showed. I was still the fastest, but I was sometimes too fast and left my center behind and ended up alone and an easy prey for a defender. I was one of the strongest in the younger group, but I could be stronger, and the development camp had highlighted what I needed to work on. I wasn't fast enough at times. At others, I was too fast. I couldn't fight the corners as well as I needed to, I needed to keep my head up. I just needed to improve on all the little things that'd make me a more rounded player.

Dad squeezed a little. "Your grades are good considering. You're refining your hockey. What's the problem?"

Academically, I didn't have to try too hard. I had inherited my Mom's freaky-ass cleverness, so I had her to thank for that. No, studying wasn't the real issue, even if I hadn't even declared a major yet nor had any idea of what I wanted to learn. No, the real question was that, even with popularity and confidence, I was lonely. I had friends, but aside from Andy, they were only interested in talking to the guy who knew Ten Rowe, not to me.

You're an idiot. There are kids out there who would give their right arm to be part of hockey royalty. Suck it the fuck up.

"No, not my studying. That's average but okay."

"Then, is it the team?" Dad prompted.

I blew out a frustrated breath. The Leicester College team wasn't really a team. It was coaches who sucked and a culture of doing the least to get by that I found frustrating. They'd said all the right things to Dad and me when we toured, but with hindsight, I think they were rubbing their hands together in glee that Ten and Dad might attend events.

"It's the hockey. The team, it's not… right."

And that was as much as I could explain. I was young, inexperienced, but I knew I could be better if I could find the right college team.

Or maybe college wasn't a good fit for me at all. Perhaps I should go professional, play for the feeder team to the Raptors, a lower level? The Raptors wanted me to work on my game, but I didn't need to be at college for that. Right? Dad would understand.

"Here's how this goes," he began. "You're a man now, okay, and this is your life. Take the summer, and we'll talk at the end of it. I can help you figure things out then. Yeah?"

Just telling Dad how I felt was enough for some of the worries to lift. "Okay, thank you."

Dad had fought Grandpa so hard to stop him from pushing me into playing professionally from the first possible day I could. He wanted me to have an education, but at the end of it all, he loved me and would listen to me. Jared Madsen was cool like that.

We hugged, awkwardly with the bags and sticks, and then I walked into the center, ready to start my summer.

I was paired up with Oslo Bruin, a short guy, maybe a little older than me, in a polo shirt emblazoned with the logo of the center. He had a quick line in summarizing everything on offer. Not slick or fawning, he didn't ask one question about my Dad or Ten, so as of right now he was my new friend. He took me into the dining hall, where it seemed I'd landed directly in the middle of breakfast, and my confident mask slid into place. The one where I was a first-round pick and had no doubts about my place in the world. Some would call it arrogance; I called it a brilliant defense mechanism. It seemed as if I was one of forty or so guys and more than a few girls, all of whom introduced themselves—as if I was ever going to remember their names. I hadn't seen Andy yet, but the text I'd gotten said he was running late over a flight mix-up. I made polite small talk, grabbed some breakfast, and then Oslo guided me out from the horde of welcoming fellow skaters to a small room off reception.

"Room allocations are random," he explained. "We like to match forwards and defense, drafted and nondrafted, building relationships, which works really well."

"So I'll be with the D or a goalie, and they'll be undrafted." I was only confirming my understanding, but Oslo narrowed his gaze.

"Is that an issue?" he asked and waited for me to say something clever.

"Not at all."

"Okay then, your roommate is Jacob Benson out of Owatonna U in Minnesota."

"Good college," I said, half because it was true and half because I felt I should be mending fences for not making it clear I was happy with anyone as a roommate. I wasn't lying,

Owatonna had been on Ten's list when he'd handed his research to me. He was another guy who hadn't done college, but the generational talents in hockey didn't do college. They went straight into playing the big leagues. When he'd handed me the information he'd found, he'd apparently spent ages checking all kinds of things out, underscored by a whole sheaf of stats that he'd commissioned for me. I'd gone with my gut, chosen Leicester, and regretted it to this day.

"…and he's been here since yesterday apparently." Oslo was still talking, and I needed to pay attention.

He didn't add what position he played, or maybe he had and I'd not heard him. I assumed as I was a right wing, that he would be a D-man or a goalie. Spending the summer with a weird-ass goalie could be kind of fun. I didn't recall his name, so I don't think we'd met on the ice in any memorable way. It's not like I knew every single college player I'd gone up against, just the ones who shone. I just knew that I wouldn't make the same mistakes here as I had in my first year in college, determined to make friends and have fun.

"You want me to show you up to your room?" Oslo asked and held out the scarlet room card.

I took it and shook my head. "I can find it."

He then handed me a folder of information, and I juggled it while picking up my bags and sticks.

"That's your schedules, meal times, opportunities, and the playoff event details. Also, Mr. Powell is out of the office for the next few days, but when he comes back, he said he wanted to touch base with you."

Okay, that made sense, with Dad being an old friend. Ethan, as I knew him, had played with Dad, and I remembered him being around when I was little. He might have bought me one of my very first junior sticks, but I couldn't remember exactly.

I took the stairs to my floor, bouncing a little in excitement, and found the room easily enough. It was right at the end of a corridor, and I flashed my pass at the handle, and the door unlocked. This was going to be like staying in a hotel for the summer, with hockey added. Win-win.

The room was empty, although my roommate had moved in. He'd taken the bed on the right side, and all evidence pointed to him being ridiculously tidy. Books stood in a neat pile on his bedside cabinet, and I checked out some of the titles. A couple of hockey autobiographies, and then others that screamed college elective subjects with obscure titles about farming and animals that made me shudder. Oh well, maybe if Jacob was a smart guy, then he could show me a way to easily work my way through another year of college.

If I went back.

I dumped my bags onto my bed and stared out of the window. From there I could see Lake Plover, the July sun shining brightly on the water, and the breeze was cool on my face. The window was open, and I leaned on the sill and leaned out to look left and right. It always paid to know your surroundings.

The lock clicked, and the door opened, and I spun to study the new arrival with a grin on my face.

Wow.

I'd lucked out in the sexy stakes, big-time. He was way taller than I was, six foot six or more, and he was built, and I mean *built*. I wouldn't have wanted to meet him on the bad side of a check into the boards. Boy, he must have worked out to get arms that muscled, and shoulders that broad, and a chest that wide or…. and I was blatantly checking him out and had lost the power of speech.

Shit. Way to freak out my new summer best friend.

"Hi," I said, still grinning, and stepped forward, holding

out my hand in welcome. "Ryker 'Mads' Madsen, Right Wing, out of Leicester College, but hopefully not for much longer."

I expected the same kind of reply. This was how hockey players introduced themselves when they were at this level. At this age, we were defined by our skills.

He shook my hand, and jeez he had one hell of a grip. I shook him off and made an exaggerated show of testing my hand for damage, still smiling and still waiting for his name. Things became awkward because he merely stared at me, his bright blue sexy, pretty eyes focused intently on my face. The scrutiny was weird. Hell, *he* was weird.

I decided it might be a good idea to repeat myself, "So, yeah, Ryker Madsen—"

"I know who you are," he said, his tone soft, then pushed his hands into his pockets. He tilted his head toward my bed. "You stay that side, I'll stay on my side, and we won't have any problems."

My mouth fell open. I'm sure it did. He went into the bathroom and shut the door, and I heard the lock engage.

And I was left standing in the middle of the room wondering what the hell had just happened? Was this Jacob? And why had he said that, and why the hell was he hiding in the bathroom?

I UNPACKED MY BAGS, put everything away as best I could, propping up the new CCM Ten-X curve stick Ten had given me by the closet, in the small space there. I took it back out and held it correctly;. It was beautiful, sleek, and so sturdy in my hands. This was from the line of sticks that Ten had worked on with CCM and had his signature in the design work.

I pushed it back in alongside my older sticks, then attempted to fit the rest of my clothes on the shelves.

Maybe all the Railers stuff was overkill. I had four Rowe jerseys from Ten, and I took them out of the closet and put them under the bed. I wouldn't wear them here, even though that was why Ten had given them to me. I wanted it to be a connection that everyone forgot.

The knock startled me out of my thoughts, and I opened the door quickly. Two of the guys from earlier, Will and James, plus one of the girls, Lois I think, stood there, grinning.

"We're heading into town to check it out. You coming?" Lois asked.

The door to the bathroom opened, and my roommate came out.

"Sounds good," I said and grabbed my wallet and room card. "You coming, Jacob?"

Jacob just stared at me.

"Oh sorry," Will said, "there's only room for one in the car."

I was torn. On the one hand, these were potential friends. On the other, I really wanted to get to know my roommate better. It seemed to me we got off on the wrong foot.

"Actually, you know what. I'm going to give it a miss this time, but next time… yeah?"

They exchanged looks but said nothing, and I closed the door to talk to Jacob.

He was on the bed flicking through a book, an open notepad and pen by his side, and very obviously didn't glance up at me.

Great. Now, what did I say? I glanced over at his sticks, saw the gorgeous lines of an old Warrior stick, and knew exactly how to break the ice.

FOUR

Jacob
_____

Super. Now I was stuck with the kid from Posh Acres. As if this city boy and I would have anything to talk about. Why hadn't he gone with the small tribe of his adoring fans?

"Nice stick. You use a Warrior just like Brady Rowe. Do you have the same flex he uses? I read his is like this insane 150-155 flex. I'm using an 80."

"That's a 130."

"I guess I better start lifting more."

That jerked my nose out of my textbook. Ryker sat down on his bed, smiling at me as if his knowledge of hockey sticks would have me fawning all over him.

"Yeah, so? You got something against that brand?"

He blinked. "Oh, uh, no man. Some of the greatest players around use Warrior sticks. You a fan of Brady's? He's a great guy. Kind of uptight—"

"Like me?" I threw that out before he could. I knew what people said and thought about me. That I was too clenched, too into the studies and not into the parties, too sullen, too uncaring about current trends and clothes. Too damn hick and way too damn poor.

Again he blinked those expressive eyes, his brows flying up under a curtain of riotous brown bangs that he'd been raking back off his face when I'd slung my reply at him.

"Okay, Jacob, I really have no idea what I've done to you in some past life, but this hostile agro shit is not cool."

I returned to my book, the *tick-tick-tick* of raindrops hitting the window from a sudden summer shower the only sound in the room.

"It's nothing to do with a past life and everything to do with your current life."

A long, painful silence fell back over us.

"I don't know what you mean," he replied, and it sounded like he was honest.

I threw him a quick glance, and yeah, he was genuinely confused. He'd dropped his bangs, and they rested on his brows, over them actually. The man was far too hot to be such a spoiled rich snot.

Slapping my textbook shut, since it was apparent no studying was going to get done, I sat up and looked right into those amazing light brown eyes of his.

"You and I are from two different worlds." He nodded as if he understood, but he didn't. How could he? "You came buzzing in here in a car that probably cost more than the second mortgage on my parents' house. I limped up here in an '89 Ford pickup that leaks more oil than an Exxon tanker, has shit suspension from hauling hay bales in it, and had the radio busted out two years ago when a calf put its hoof through the dash. Can you see where I'm going here?"

"You had a cow in your truck?"

Now it was my time to blink stupidly. Out of all that, he noticed toting a calf in the cab of my truck?

"It was a calf, not a cow, and the point I was making was—"

He leaned in, putting his elbows on the knees of his jeans, all that hair falling forward to frame a face too pretty for any man.

"You had a baby cow—calf—in your truck?"

"Yeah, I was taking it to a fellow FFA member's farm for his baby brother to raise, and my friend lost control of the calf midway to his farm. The point I was trying to make was—"

"So this guy was holding a baby cow on his lap?"

Okay, was this guy slow-witted or what? "Yes, he had the calf on his lap. We do it all the time."

"I have never even seen a baby cow—calf—up close. Where do you live? On a farm, I figured out. Do you have cows? Do you milk them? What other kinds of animals do you have? Do you have a dog? Like a cow dog? I have little sisters who would love to come visit your farm!"

His enthusiasm stunned me into silence. This was not the way he was supposed to react. He was supposed to laugh at my cow-wrangler status, make fun of my stupid hair and worn-out jeans, and then run off to hang out with the players who were more like him.

"Uhm, I live in a small farming town named Eden Crossing, in Minnesota."

"Ah, cool. You have an accent. It's nice." He smiled. He needed to stop smiling because it made him cute and approachable, and his dimple came into play when he smiled.

"Right, uh, thanks? So, yeah we milk them. We have chickens. No dog, not now. We had one, Lincoln, but he got old and died last year, and good herding dogs are expensive, so we never replaced him." Fuck, now I was under siege with memories of Lincoln, our black-and-white border collie. He had been my best friend, the only one on the farm whom I could talk to without reserve when I'd been trying to come to grips with my sexuality. Linc never judged; he just loved. I'd really needed that when the Dirk thing had come to light.

"Sorry about your dog."

I shook off the recollections and found that Ryker Madsen appeared to be genuinely upset about my loss.

"It was only a dog." Oh no, that was my father talking. Nope. "I mean, no, he was a great dog. Nothing gets cows moving faster than a dog nipping at them. Back when we were running some beefers to try to help cover the shrinking milk checks, he'd bring those big bastards in from pasture slicker than anything. My father trained him."

"Cool. Maybe you'll get a new dog soon."

"Not likely. We don't have beef cattle anymore. We're back to strictly dairy."

"Ah, well, you could have a dog just for the sake of having a dog, yeah?" Ryker seemed interested in all of this, but why? Why would he care about a dog and me? It made no sense.

"Not going to happen. Everything on a farm has to earn its keep." I pushed down the feeling that this guy might not be as much of a dick as I'd assumed, despite his fancy sneakers and a gold watch. "Look, I'm trying to grab some study time so can you just—"

"Why are you studying over summer break?"

Okay, this guy was making my head spin. "Are you always this fucking nosy?"

That made him laugh. It was a warm sound, honest. "I'm just trying to figure you out, Jacob. We're going to be in this room together for a month. If we can see where the other is coming from, we can avoid all kinds of upset and shit in the future. So, tell me why you're studying when you should be all about the hockey camp."

Right. Like I was going to tell this guy about my crushing

need to graduate—early if at all possible so I could get back to the farm sooner—and have him make fun of me. *Not happening.*

"Let's just say my daddy can't buy me a place on campus. I have to work for it." I snapped up my book, papers, and pen, and left the room with him gaping at my back.

I found a small couch down the hall, next to the ice machine, threw myself onto it, and spent several hours reading up on crop insurance and record keeping. By midnight I was ready to cram my head into the ice machine to end my suffering. Sneaking back into the room I shared with Ryker, I discovered he was sound asleep and he snored in this soft little princess way. It was cute. Not cute like cute but cute like... well, hell.

I stripped quickly and dove into bed, eager for sleep to take me before I mentally found more cute things about Ryker Madsen.

THE INFO in the brochures about the intensity of this camp hadn't lied. From that first day after we'd all arrived, we were worked hard. And by hard, I mean insanely hard. The program was one short step away from killing me, and I had always considered myself a rugged guy. Years of manual labor, combined with all the requirements for NCAA hockey seemed like a pixie dance compared to the rigors of the Rayzor Edge Performance regime.

Within two days, I ached in places I didn't know a man could hurt. The staff was relentless, loud, demanding, but never rude or demeaning. They pushed us hard every day, making us lift more, run longer, skate harder, work faster. A weaker man would have left after the first torturous day, but I was not a weak man. I had to endure, get stronger and faster.

Especially faster because I was slow and I knew it. Most D-men aren't whippets on the ice, not like the forwards. It just stood to reason that someone my size—six-six and usually around two hundred and fifty pounds—was not going to be a speed demon. Defensemen used to be given some slack back in the day for their lack of speed. In today's game? No quarter was given because the forwards had gotten faster, so we had to as well.

Today's funfest was all about working with the speed chutes. I stood on the ice among my fellow defensemen, arms up, as the defensive coach, a whiskery old Boston alum who liked to be called Headless for some unknown reason—probably because back in his day he took the heads off of his opponents—strapped me into a four-foot round parachute which would add wind resistance to our morning skate.

"This is truly going to suck, my man," Zach mumbled.

I nodded in dull silence. Zach Dean was my defensive buddy, paired up with me during my rookie season last year. He was a year older now, a junior this fall, and had this funny sort of California way of looking at things. Shorter than me by about five inches, blond as a surfing god, and stocky.

"Welcome to my life." Headless snugged the straps tightly around my chest, gave me an evil grin that was nearly obscured by the fat walrus mustache on his upper lip.

Zach and I, our chutes dragging behind us, skated out to join the others waiting at the home end of the ice. The nets had been removed, and even the goalies were out there with us, Ben jawing at me about how the staff had taken his bottle of Canadian water from him. This was a massive outrage and total mojo mess-up because Ben—the goalie that he was—always took water from his hometown and sprinkled it onto the blue paint. Then he would dig it up with his skates, mixing the inferior American ice with his glorious Quebec ice until the little rows of icy powder suited him. This could, at times, take up to ten minutes.

Goalies are just plain weird.

"…use this water! I'm sure this water has nasty chemicals that will make the ice less dense," Ben was muttering angrily, his accent a bit deeper when he was angry.

"Dude, just pretend the ice is light." Zach gave Ben his best airy smile.

Ben gave me a look. I shrugged.

"You can't pretend the ice is light. I need another goalie. Sam!" He found Sam Gagnon, our backup, also a Canadian, among the players waiting for chutes. Off Ben went to bend Sam's ear.

I was about to ask Zach just how much pot he had smoked in his past, but whistles blew, and our names were called. Headless barked at us to go when he dropped his arm. Stick in hand, I hunkered down, ready to show them something. As soon as Headless dropped his arm, I powered off and immediately felt the tug of the chute slowing me down. Zach and I slugged along, hitting the first mark at the blue line, changing direction, touching back where we started, and then heading to the other end of the ice before repeating the whole thing again.

We caught our breath while the other defensive pairs had their turns. Then we went again and again and again. The forwards joined us, coming to the ice after a run around the lake. Ryker Madsen looked as if he'd been run through a baler. I felt as if I'd been, and our jog was yet to come.

We'd not talked much over the past couple of days, mainly because by the time we got back to our room, we were too tired to do anything but grunt at each other. Or in my case, ogling his ass through the cracked bathroom door as he stepped into the shower. Then we fell into bed after the light was out to sleep the sleep of the dead.

"This as much fun as it looks?" Ryker asked, skating up to me as I tried to suck in enough air to counter the need to pass out.

"Tons," I huffed.

He snorted, clapped my back, and then went to get his chute on. Knowing that in a week we'd be playing a scrimmage game with these chutes on our backs made me seriously consider jumping into the old red Ford and going home. But the fee was nonrefundable, and I had to stick with it or be cut come fall.

"That dude there is killer sweet," Zach announced, his bright blue eyes locked on Ryker.

"You mean on the ice?"

"I mean just on the planet, dude."

That made me snap out of my funk a bit. I looked down on my defensive partner. "Are you gay?"

"I do dudes, especially dudes with hair like that. You think Madsen would join me in my room for a pizza and a blow job?"

"Uhm."

"Oh dude, were you into him?"

The team knew I was gay. There had never been any issue with that at all, which was one of the joyous things about being on campus. I could walk the quad to class and not get looks as I did back in Eden Crossing. Being the only gay man in a conservative town was uncomfortable, to say the least. On the Owatonna U campus, I was one of many LGBT students. Hell, we even had our own dorm, an activist group, and a big Pride festival the week before finals.

"Right. Like I'd be into someone like him." I rolled my eyes.

"Is he open to dudes?"

"How should I know?"

"You're sleeping with him."

"I'm not sleeping with him. We're in the same room. We barely talk. He's too... too uppity. I can barely stand him. And he is certainly not my type."

"What is your type?"

I skated away from Zach before the conversation dipped into a place it didn't need to go. I removed the chute, tossed it to Headless, and went to sit on the bench, my legs still rubbery. My gaze moved to Ryker Madsen, chewing up that chute skate. Man, he was much faster than me, faster than most of the other forwards out there with him. Trying to defend against him was going to be tough. I wondered if Tennant Rowe was guiding him along. Probably. That kid had it all. Really, it was beyond unfair.

My type. Sure. As if. Pfft. If I had a type, which I really didn't, because who had time for romance when you carried the family future on your shoulders, but if I did have a type, it wouldn't be—

Was Zach over there hitting on Ryker? Really? For fuck sake, he was. Okay, that was total bullshit! How did he get Ryker to smile like that? Shit, that smile was incredible, and that dimple. Fucking Zach and his Cali appeal. If he ended up with Madsen, I'd be... happy as hell because Ryker Madsen was absolutely *not* my type.

FIVE

Ryker

I NOTICED THAT, WHEN WE HAD ANY DOWNTIME, JACOB would withdraw from the team bantering while killing time shooting hoops. Thirty minutes here or there, and he would vanish from sight. Not that I was watching him all the time. Just *most* of the time. He always had a bag with him, and I knew what was in there, books. Dry technical manuals about farming, or I assume they were connected to his subject. I had read the back of one of them which promised exciting information about some sort of technical thing.

I guess it was no different to me reading up on hockey technique. Not that I did a lot of that. Reading rather than doing bored me to tears. I'd preferred being out on the ice learning from Ten or watching the Railers to studying angles and plays in a book. Then again, my degree didn't depend on knowing the mathematics of hockey or the kinesiology of a skater.

Jacob didn't look bored when he was reading his books, though. He always had this faint smile on his face, as if he was enjoying every word. Well, most of the time, unless he frowned, which is when he'd pull out his yellow highlighter and make sweeping motions over certain parts of the text.

Okay, so maybe I *had* been spending too much time watching him.

I followed him down the stairs but was waylaid by Oslo who wanted to talk jerseys and sizes. I tried to listen, but I was pleased when he waved me away and told me I was too scattered today.

I jogged to the front step, looked for any sign of the big man who could disappear so easily. Following my instinct, knowing he was searching for a quiet place to study, I went to the lake. I felt a distinct twinge of guilt that my sole purpose was tracking him down and making his quiet place noisy, but it was just this once. What could thirty minutes hurt?

I found him easily. He was kind of hard to miss. He was propped up against a tree, a pen in his mouth, and one of his books open on his lap. His long legs were stretched in front of him, and he was hunched a little, peering down at the text.

"You'll end up with bad shoulders," I said.

He looked right up at me, startled at first, and then resigned. "Go away," he said and went back at his book.

"Can I sit?" I was good at this ignoring business, and I wasn't going to be deterred.

"Go away."

I sat anyway.

He let out a huff of irritation. "What don't you understand about the words go and away?"

"I have a question for you," I forged ahead, not wanting to give Jacob a moment in which he felt he could make me leave. Dad called me tenacious, Mom said I was a pain in the ass, Ten just laughed at me, but I generally got my way.

"Unless it's about the place of farm animals in sustainable agriculture, then go away."

"Is that one of your subjects? Do you actually need to study in the summer break? I don't have anything I need to study."

He closed his eyes briefly, and I could tell he was reining in the need to punch me or something equally physical. Nothing new for a hockey player. When he opened them again, I was blown away by how gorgeous they were. Was it wrong to call a man's eyes pretty? They were the most incredible shade of blue and framed by the thickest lashes. I swear he had a few freckles across his cheekbones, and I leaned closer to have a better look.

"What the fuck?" Jacob snapped and shut his book firmly. "What is wrong with you?"

"Nothing." I scooted back a little. "I just want to know what you're doing, why you study on all the breaks, and why you won't come out with us?"

Three times now, Jacob had been included in events. Pizza had been last night and the latest group outing he'd turned down. Each time he'd said no, and I had an issue with that. Hockey was about team. It was about learning each other and listening and laughing and building camaraderie. None of which Jacob was actually doing. He was a solid player on the ice, a brick wall when he needed to be, could be better on his skates at times, a bit slow in the corners, and he certainly wasn't draft material. But he was good. He just needed to learn how to be a bigger part of the team.

Jacob regarded me steadily and then shook his head.

"Go away," he snapped, then opened his book.

"No one here knows you," I countered, desperate to get some kind of connection. I shuffled forward again and laid a hand on the book, which was open at a page of a goat mounting another goat. Then I tried for my best serious tone.

"Jacob, you can't be one of the team unless you know the team."

Jacob made a noise of derision. "You read that in a cookie, Madsen?"

I was confused and went back over what he'd said; everything I'd said was true. Maybe Jacob didn't understand the profoundness of my statement. Was profoundness even a word? Profundity? Something like that.

"What I mean by that is—"

Jacob held up a hand. "I know what you meant, but actually the *team* and I get on just fine. It's you they don't know, Mr. Bigshot-on campus-asshole."

My chest felt suddenly tight, an unfamiliar poke of pain that made no sense at first, but then I realized it was hurt. His label of what I was hurt me. There had been genuine dislike in his words, and I couldn't understand where the hostility was coming from. I'd tried so hard to be nice to Jacob, even imagined we could be friends one day, but clearly Jacob wasn't won over by me.

"I'm not what you said," I defended himself.

"Yeah, asshole, you are. Now for the last freaking time. Go. Away."

"I just wanted…" I stopped when Jacob's eyes went back to his book. He'd dismissed me.

"Jeez, I know when I'm not wanted, asshole," I snapped and left him to his isolated seating spot. I was pissed at him, and that stayed with me until I got back to the building. What the hell had just happened?

People wanted to be my friend; that was how things worked. And I'd been approaching Jacob for *real* reasons, not just to annoy him.

At Leicester College, I had a huge group of friends, people who wanted to have pizza with me and talk to me. I took some deep breaths, that feeling of uncertainty still in my chest, and thought about the next session. I'd promised to work with Scott on passes, and that was what teamwork was all about. It was me sharing my knowledge with people who didn't have my luck in life. Not that I knew if Scott hadn't had luck, but I was channeling my worry about Jacob. I knew that.

But people expected things from me. I had a responsibility. Why couldn't Jacob see that?

"Ryker!"

I turned to find Lois, Will and James on the steps. They were the social organizers, the ones who were trying hard to build friendships in the team. Each of them came from hockey families like mine. Each of them had futures set in stone, with NHL and NWHL journeys of their own. After turning them down that first day, I'd gone along with whatever they planned, but at no point did they include Jacob, and maybe I was still pissed from Jacob telling me to leave, but I felt antsy.

"Hey," I said and crossed to stand with them, "what's up?"

Lois stepped into my space. She did that a lot, and as she was a step above me, we were face-to-face, and I could see her green eyes. She was a good player, one of seven girls here and aiming for the US women's development team. She smiled at me and placed a hand on my arm.

"James found this awesome bar, three towns over. We thought we'd go tonight."

"Everyone?"

I turned when I heard someone come up the steps behind me. Jacob.

Lois shook her head subtly and then tilted it in Jacob's

direction. "Not everyone," she murmured. "Only the fun ones."

Jacob hunched over then. He must have heard what she said, and I wish I'd said something right then, but I was still pissed. Only after he glanced back at me did the guilt start, and boy did it hit me hard.

"I can't tonight," I said. "Sorry guys."

I caught up with Jacob in the corridor outside our room. I'd gone up for my stick, but it seemed like, yet again, I ended up in Jacob's quiet place.

"Are you following me?" he asked and shoved his way into the room.

"No, I need my…" I reached into the space and pulled out my stick, never taking my eyes off him. "I'm not going out with them," I explained.

He placed the book with the goats in it on top of the pile and made some kind of notation on a sheet of paper that was tucked inside a notebook.

"Doesn't bother me if you do, doesn't bother me if you don't."

I didn't know what to say. It wasn't that I was lost for words. If anything, I had too many words in my head, along with residual guilt and some of my famous temper, and I rounded on him, poking him hard in his chest.

His hard chest.

"You're rude," I snapped.

He grabbed my hand and held it tight, yanking me toward him. "Says the man who won't leave me alone."

I was way too close to him. I could smell him, a mix of soap and *Jacob*. I swear I whimpered in my head. Because I was this close to him, and he was big, *way big,* and growly, and had my hand in a grip I didn't want to pull away from. If I'd gone right up on tiptoes, I could've kissed him. He was that close to me. I even flexed my muscles ready to do just that when he shoved me away.

"Go away," he muttered and turned back to his notebook.

I could've talked more then, pushed him to interact, get my fill of all the intriguing details that made up Jacob, but I didn't.

"I don't understand your problem."

He closed his book with exaggerated patience. "You don't get it, do you? Those people aren't your friends. They just want to be with you for who you know. It's all about your connection to the Railers and your hockey superstar friend Ten around here, or haven't you noticed that?"

"I have friends that like me for me."

"No, Ryker, you really don't. You wouldn't know a real friend if you tried. Look at Scott."

"What about Scott?"

"He was talking to you yesterday, and you blew him off when you remembered a funny story about Ten buying you some gift for Christmas and how you could sell it on eBay for a couple thousand. You were telling the story, and you made people laugh, but what about Scott?"

"I'm going to work with Scott now."

"Yeah, well, don't get sidetracked with your life and how wonderful it is."

I was left speechless. He was an asshole, and I couldn't handle his shit right now. It served me right for trying to be nice to the guy and worrying about him spending too much time on his own.

I left, making sure to slam the door behind me because it felt good. I went to the sports hall, intending to talk to Scott and show him what he needed. Only, when someone pointed at me and crossed to my side, making these weird sounds and gesticulating wildly, I realized I had seriously fucked up. I'd pulled Ten's stick out without thinking. The wildly expensive stick with the signature and the custom flex, and abruptly I was a celebrity again, and friends of all kinds grouped around me to look and ask questions.

I should have been happy. I was popular, and the guys liked me, and I was right in the center of everything.

But I wasn't happy. I felt something else. Did I feel sad? Unhappy? Weird? I genuinely had no idea what to call this feeling that gripped me and made me hate being the person everyone wanted to stare at or talk to, but when I caught sight of Jacob crossing to the theory classroom for the next session, I knew I certainly felt one thing.

I felt confused.

THERE WAS an informal curfew at Rayzor Edge that wasn't written in stone. It had been explained to us that we were adults and if we wanted to be better players lack of sleep was going to mess with that. Apparently, it was our decision what we did, and no one was going to get thrown out of the program for being back from town late.

Of course, they didn't mention alcohol, and they might have had issues with the fact I couldn't walk in a straight line. The drink was good, and the need to get drunk tonight strong.

Scott and I had worked hard on our passes. We'd achieved a lot, and he'd high-fived me, and I almost asked him if I'd pissed him off with my Ten story.

Stupid Jacob with his blue eyes and his chest, making me doubt myself, making me think I was a bad person. Just because I had a dad who played hockey, and a grandad, and a great-grandad didn't mean my life was easy. My parents divorced. That was hard.

At least I was sure it was hard. I didn't remember much

about it, but I knew that Mom and Dad would have been miserable together and that they were happier with their new partners.

It wasn't hard, idiot.

And look at me now. I had two happy families, and when I ignored my interfering grandad, things were perfect.

I wasn't a bad person. I was a good person people wanted to talk to, and I was utterly determined to tell Jacob this in person. Thank god for the key card. I wasn't sure I could've worked out how to use an old-fashioned key at that moment. I stumbled into our room, and it was dark, and I settled on the side of Jacob's bed, unfortunately misjudging the fact he was a freaking giant, and landed right on his feet. He sat bolt upright, yanking himself away and cursing.

"What the fuck, Madsen?"

"What is wrong with you that you're so rude to me?" I blurted the question out and almost fell off the bed in the process. I didn't usually drink much. My body is a temple and all that, and it seemed like three beers in and I was a stupid, uncoordinated ass. He caught me as I tumbled, and I pushed with my foot on the floor to get back on his bed, up on my knees, looming over him. "What is wrong with me?" I added the second part of my question.

"What's wrong with you is that you're drunk. Go to bed."

"I'm not drunk," I said in what I hoped was my best nondrunk tone. "And I meant, what is wrong with me!" I thumped my chest then and winced when I hurt myself.

"Son of a—" Jacob got out of bed and picked me up and pushed me onto my bed. "Stay there."

I rolled to sit up. I had questions, dammit, but he placed one meaty hand right in the center of my chest, and I was like a pinned bug.

I had to say it again. "What is wrong with *me*?" I was all

over the freaking place, wondering about friends, and who liked me, and who didn't.

And why. Always why.

"Nothing. At least nothing that a dose of reality wouldn't fix," Jacob growled. "Now, stay." He pressed me hard to the mattress, then vanished into our small bathroom. Was he going to have a shower? I kind of hoped so because the door was wide open, and maybe I'd get to see more of Jacob. More ass, more of his thighs, more of his chest. He came out with a glass of water and dug into his bag. He pulled out a bottle of aspirin which he then held out to me. "Take these."

I did what I was told.

"Are you going to take a shower?" I asked and laid my head back on the pillow, the coolness of it welcoming, and its softness cradling my head.

"What?" He stepped away and sat on his bed. "I was in bed. It's midnight, you idiot."

"So that's a no then."

"Yes. No." He shook his head. "Yes, it's a no."

"Shame." I closed my eyes to attempt to stop the room from spinning. Then I thought about what I should say, that I wanted to watch, and I might have said it, or it might have still been in my head. I couldn't work it out, and I was too tired to try.

I rolled onto my side, and away from him, and closed my eyes.

"You're an idiot, Madsen," Jacob said and then pulled a blanket up and over me.

I didn't have much to say after that. It turned out alcohol not only allowed me to say stupid things, but it was also helpful in getting a person to sleep.

SIX

Jacob

I COULD FEEL HIS GAZE ON ME. ODDLY ENOUGH, I WAS NOW getting used to it. To say the truth, when he wasn't studying me like some new and exotic species of bug the scientific community had just discovered, something inside me began seeking his attention, wondering where it was and why he wasn't looking at me. It was moronic and confusing and made me mad and edgy. Yet even as the tumbling mosh of conflicting emotions mowed me down like standing hay, I glanced up from my textbook to find Ryker smiling softly at me.

"What?"

He threw his feet from his bed, put his elbows on his knees, and smiled even wider, his eyes glowing and intense, yet utterly beautiful.

"You remind me of the first guy I ever kissed. He used to do that 'tongue between the teeth' thing that you do when you're concentrating."

I had no reply to that. If the man had hit me in the face with a brick, I would have been less stunned.

"You're gay?" I asked, my book sort of sliding from my lap to the bed, then closing.

When he shook his head, all that thick hair slithered back and forth, the sun making it shine. Must be that fancy shampoo he used.

"Bi. Pretty sure I'm bi."

I had to make some spit, then quickly swallow it. All this time I'd shoved the lust down deep because Ryker Madsen *had* to be straight. He had to be; otherwise the sex dreams I'd been having for the past four nights might have had a slim chance of coming true.

"So, you don't know?"

He sat up straight and lifted a shoulder. "I mean, yeah, I know. I think." He hit me with a quirky smile, one that I'd seen him flash a hundred times over the past couple of weeks, mostly at girls. "It's not so easy finding out who you are sexually, is it?"

"It was for me." I grabbed my book, found my page, and read the same line ten times before the silence compelled me to speak.

He was sitting there, working that smile, waiting, the thin strap of his tank top resting on his biceps, baring the left side of his neck and shoulder. It was driving me fucking nuts seeing that span of exposed skin. I laid my book over my dick, hoping it would hide the raging hard-on. "I knew I was gay when I was twelve."

"That's cool." Our gazes locked over the two feet of distance between his bed and mine. "If you're willing, can I tell you something personal?"

Fuck. Shit fuck, no, do not tell me that you want to crawl into my bed and let me peel you out of that dusky blue Railers tank because... well, just don't.

I nodded, since talking was not advisable right now. God knows what sort of stupidity would flow out of me.

"You're a good skater, but you could be better."

I blinked like a cow that had just run into the electric fencing. "Oh, okay."

He left his bed, then sat beside me, his hip tight to my thigh. Denim to flesh. There was no wriggle room. The stupid bed was barely wide enough for me.

"And I'm not trying to impress you with my shit because I know you think I'm some sort of show-off, flashy ass, but I've been watching you."

"I know."

His gaze grew a little smoky. I pressed down harder on the book resting on my cock. It kind of hurt, but it also kind of felt good. Fuck this guy and his mouth and eyes and all that hair. Christ, he was waiting for a reply. Had he said something?

"Whatever." There, that covered all the bases.

"Cool. So, Ten taught me this trick to help with your speed. You're a good skater, superstrong, but you're way too slow. I think I can help you, if you want… I mean, if you're willing to let me show you a few tricks." He stared at me earnestly, his blue eyes reading me like the book on my lap.

My first reaction was to say no, go away, fuck off. But as I slipped and slewed around in his eyes, I felt myself easing back a bit. I *did* need to speed up if I wanted to stay on the team. And if he had tips from Tennant Rowe, what kind of an ass would I be not to try to implement them? My future—and the farm's future—rode on my staying on the team.

"Okay, yeah, sure."

His smile blossomed into a grin. I shoved my elbow into my text book as my pulse throbbed in my dick.

"Cool! We'll meet up tonight after everyone else is off

doing stupid shit like getting drunk." He leapt off the bed. My thigh instantly missed his warmth. "I'm going to go for a run. You want to come?"

"No, I need to study."

"Ah man, you spend far too much time with your face in a book." He slapped the bottom of my bare foot playfully, then stripped down to his underwear, tossing his clothes into the air. I watched closely, enjoying the way his muscles moved and how graceful he was, how his lean but firm body folded when he bent down to find his running shoes under the bed. I had to close my eyes to avoid seeing those shorts pull tightly over his ass as he searched for his sneakers. "Man, someone needs to tidy up this room."

"You mean someone needs to tidy up *that* side of the room. My side's clean."

He sat back on his heels, hair hanging into his face, and slapped me with another killer smile.

"Yeah, I'm a fucking slob. It's part of my charm."

"Totally not a charming trait," I replied.

He laughed, pulled on his clothes and shoes, and made a dash for the door.

"So, you sure you're not coming?" he asked, pausing inside the doorframe.

I slapped my book and nearly groaned aloud. "Nope, work to do. Go away now."

Ryker rapped on the frame, gave me a wink, and left me alone to study. Study, right now, meaning jerking off. I couldn't get my hand into my shorts fast enough. My Farm Management and Operations book fell to the floor with a loud *thunk* that barely registered. I grabbed my cock and stroked it hard and fast, closing my eyes so that I could pull up some erotic fantasy such as Ryker on his knees, my dick in his mouth—the mouth that kissed men—and my fingers wound in that rich, long, dark hair of his. The tingle in my balls came out of nowhere and shot to the base of my spine. With a growl, I came like a bull, pumping into my hand, guttural sounds rolling out of me, the mental image of Ryker Madsen swallowing my load tripling the intensity of the orgasm.

"Oh… fuck, holy fuck," I panted, working my dick until I was done, then, carefully, pulling my hand out of my shorts to gaze at the spunk coating my fingers and palm. "Shit," I huffed, my legs wobbly as I got off the bed and entered the bathroom to look at myself in the round mirror over the sink. Yep, that was the face of a man who had just tugged one off over some guy he hated. Hated. Disliked. Envied maybe? "Shit," I said again as I washed off the signs of all my Ryker Madsen hatred.

"OKAY, so the first thing you need to do is learn how to use your edges better."

I cocked an eyebrow at Ryker. The rink was all ours. It was close to midnight. How he had wrangled this time on the ice was beyond me. I was sure it had something to do with his last name, but whatever. If him throwing his famous name around helped me stay on the team, maybe I should try not to be such a large, tired sack of dicks.

We should've been in bed sleeping because tomorrow was already being touted as a day spent outside running with weights dragging behind us. What fun. Woot. Fuck my life right now.

"How exactly?" I shifted my weight from one skate to the other, my helmet resting loosely on my head. Ryker had his strapped on. His flow was epic. I was so jealous of that hair. My father would've passed a kidney if I'd let my hair grow that long. He commented on it when it touched my collar.

"See, here's the thing. When you skate, your skate is straight up and down, which is great for gliding, but if you want real speed and power, you need to get off the flat of your blade and roll your ankles in or out more deeply."

"Show me."

"Sure." He then demonstrated how to ramp up my acceleration out of the corners, which would keep me closer to the faster forwards. "Dig into the ice with your edge more! You've got thighs like fucking tree trunks. Use all those muscles!" he shouted as I practiced exploding from a stop using more of my skate edges. "No, you're back to spinning your wheels again. Dig in with the edge. Yeah, better! Okay, now see if you can stay with me."

He was fast. Way faster than me, but with the short little workout and utilizing my edges better, I could close the gap a little more quickly.

"Sweet! You're going to be a rocket by the time this camp is over. You want to work on some speed drills?"

"Yeah, sure."

For the next ten minutes, we were all about the drills. We'd lie on our stomachs, then push up to our feet and streak down the ice. Ryker beat me every time. I mean, like every damn time. Then we did some backpedal sprints, then a couple of sets of resistance sprints with Ryker holding onto a band that went around my waist while I skated down the ice. He might have been smaller than me, but pulling his weight was exhausting.

"Had enough?" he asked when I fell over the boards at the end of the last resistance sprint.

"I'm done," I huffed and lay there like a wet blanket. Ryker chuckled, grabbed a leg, and hoisted it over the boards. Then he flung my left leg over. I threw myself onto the bench, my eyes on the rafters, my lungs burning. "You need a diet."

"Nah, *you* just need to get stronger." He sat, his hip sliding over the crown of my head. "I'm not sure how much bigger you can get though. I've seen you lift. You're already massive. Hey, maybe you need to slim it down a bit instead of bulking."

"Yeah… maybe."

"Could work. I mean, you're huge, heavy. You could probably drop twenty and still be as big and strong, but that would be less poundage to cart up and down the ice."

"Yeah, possibly." I was too spent to think about future scenarios. All I wanted at that moment was oxygen, some water, and a shower. Ryker shifted a bit on the bench, easing himself closer to me, sliding his thigh under my head. I stiffened a bit at the intimate way the back of my skull was now resting on his thigh. If I'd rolled my head to the left, my nose would've been right in his hockey pants, which was not at all erotic, yet I was getting strangely turned on by the thought of rubbing my face against the padded pants. Fuck sake, this was getting out of hand. I went to sit up, but he placed his palm, which was as sweaty as my brow, to my forehead, keeping me where I was.

"Just rest there, man. Bench is hard."

"Why are you doing this?" I asked, my throat dry and my voice weak.

"Because you've made me think about me, who I am, where I come from, you know, inner reflections and all that." He glanced down at me. There were lots of thoughts skipping around behind his eyes. "I guess I never really knew how privileged I was. I mean, I did but not really. Not until I saw myself through someone else's eyes."

"Some of that might have been my own envy." I had to

say something to him to lift some of the weight off his shoulders. "First time I saw you and your dad in that fancy car with the top-of-the-line gear, I was jealous." I sighed and let my eyes drift shut. "We're struggling to make ends meet on the farm, and that's not on you, it's just the way it is. I've lived my whole life wearing secondhand clothes, driving shit cars, working from sunup to sundown just to help keep food on the table, and when I see people like you, fighting for every break and every miserable grant or endowment…well, people like you remind me of how poor I really am. It cuts, you know? Because why the hell should you have all the breaks while my family can't pay the mortgage."

My pity party message floated up into the girders. It was so quiet there on the bench that I could hear my heart beating.

Ryker's fingers moved over my brow, a soft little caress that I think had been meant to be something less sensual and more comforting. Hell, who knew what either of us meant? I opened my eyes and found his gaze resting on my face.

"I don't think any less of you because you're not as… well off as we are. I think you working hard to get where you are is admirable. Like, I've had everything pretty much handed to me when I asked, hell sometimes before. I got tickets to go see my favorite rock band up in Canada for my birthday. I mean, that was a great gift, but man was it over the top." He sighed. His fingers drifted into my hair, which was wet and gross from hockey, but he didn't seem to care.

"Yeah, that's about as over the top as a kid can get."

He winced at the bite in my tone. "I know. So, you opened up a new way of thinking for me. Thanks for that."

His fingertips moved through my hair. My heart began to kick and flutter.

"Kiss me in thanks," I whispered.

His sexy eyes flared for a second, just a second, and then

he bent and pressed his mouth over mine. I'd been kissed a few times before, of course, Dirk being the first, but this kiss... Ah, God above, this kiss, even closed-mouthed, was magic. It filled my head and body with heat and cinnamon toast sweetness. Without realizing, I reached up, cupped the back of his sweaty neck, and held his lips to mine. Ryker's breath left his nose in a rush of warm air. Somehow, I managed to keep my mouth on his as I sat up. There was this small moment—just when we had to break apart as sanity tried its best to kick lust the hell out of the way—when we were sitting there staring at each other. His lips were slightly parted, all that glorious hair of his damp and flat to his skull, his eyes hot and hooded.

"I want more thanks," I managed to cough out before I moved, capturing his mouth with mine and pressing him back to the bench.

He opened for me, the tip of his tongue meeting mine, then sliding over it. Madness. Yes, this was fucking insanity, but there was no stopping it. His hands went under my sweater, skipping over my ribs and shoulder pads as I kissed him hard and deep. There was too much between us. I needed to feel him against me. That would've been insane. I knew it. Some small voice inside my head knew it too, so I lay on top of him and began grinding into him.

"Ah, shit, fuck..." He sounded winded, but I think it was passion that made him breathless.

I had to free my cock from my cup. I reached into my pants at the same time he did, and then I gyrated against him as he yanked my mouth back to his. Dick freed now, I could at least get some sensation. He arched up, his skates planted on the matting, my knee on the bench. I lapped at his mouth, then rotated my hips, my ass clenching as my orgasm tickled my nuts. Ryker came first, his teeth on my throat, his hands on my well-padded ass. He made soft, harsh sounds as he blew his nut. I'd never heard anything like them before. They made me whimper and thrust and come so powerfully I saw black spots floating in front of me.

Once the madness abated, we were lying there, me draped over him, his hands on my sides, my lips roaming along his jaw.

"I like late night drills," he whispered. I grunted in amusement, then lifted my head so I could see into him. "That was kind of…"

"Yeah, it was kind of that."

He was so pretty lying under me. I wanted more. More of this, only with a lot fewer clothes.

"So uhm, where does this go from here?" he asked and gave me a gentle push. When I was standing, he drew in a long, deep breath, then sat up. "Ugh man, my pants are a mess."

"Mine too." I took a lock of his hair and rubbed it between my fingers. "I guess this goes to the locker room and showers."

"Well, yeah, but I kind of meant after we wash the cum off." He stood.

I liked that I was taller than him. I was starting to like a lot about the guy whom I hated. My head was a mess, but my body knew what was what. "We go back to our room and go to bed."

He nodded, rose to grab a kiss, and then thumped off to the showers. I sat back down, stared at the ice, and gave him all the time he might've needed to wash up without me there ogling him. I needed to sort out my thoughts and all those preconceived notions.

An hour later I stepped into our room. The light was out. I stepped softly over the clothes and shit scattered on his side, then sat to take off what I was wearing. I heard him sigh as I tugged off my shirt. I let the old cotton tee fall to the floor, then stood to take off my jeans. Once back in bed, I rolled to face him in the dark.

"You okay? With everything?"

"Yeah." There was a slight pause. "You?"

"I'm good, mostly. You know we have nine days left here, and then we'll never see each other again. It would be stupid to start something."

"I know, but man, I would *love* to start something."

"Me too."

We both remained silent. It took him a long time to fall asleep. I never did.

SEVEN

Ryker

DAD ALWAYS SAID I COULD SLEEP ANYWHERE. WHEN I WAS A toddler, apparently I would fall asleep face first in my cereal bowl at the drop of a hat. There's a picture on Mom's wall of me, aged three, snoozing with my head in my cereal bowl, still clutching my tiny hockey stick. The stick had been a present from Dad, and it had come with a small net and some soft balls. I remember it clearly and had shot some of my finest goals with that stick.

I slept with it all the time, and I still have it, or rather Mom has it in a box she keeps for me. The box is labeled with *RYKER* in bright primary colors that she drew and I colored in when I was seven. Inside, is the tiny stick, along with the puck from Dad's first goal, various photos, and an old ratty blanket.

It's blue and gold, which were the colors of my Dad's first team in Buffalo.

Sleeping with my stick and my blanket was a comfort thing. I didn't like pacifiers or teddies. Nope, I was all about the stick and that blanket.

Right now though, I'd decided that Jacob was my new

best thing when it came to comfort. I was tired, and maybe it was because we were losing sleep with too much kissing and hand jobs. Or it could've been due to the fact he was so easy to hug. Whatever it was, I knew lying with my head in Jacob's lap as he studied and dozing off on his thigh was wonderful.

"Ryker? Ryker? Ryker!"

He shook me, and I turned my face to his body, nose to groin, and then grinned up at him.

"Kiss?" I asked, hopeful he'd take pity on me. He already tolerated a lot from me. I mean, I was in the way of his books, which he'd taken to resting on my head. At that moment, he was studying advances in biotechnology or something equally clever. I would swear that wasn't on his course. It all looked way too complicated and didn't have a single picture of a goat or a cow.

"No time for kisses." He closed the book.

"There's always time for kisses."

"Not right now."

"I love it when you're serious."

He sighed noisily. "We need to get downstairs," He shook me again, this time a lot harder; it seemed as if he *really* didn't want to spend time kissing.

I was only teasing really, we had a class to get to, and I had to admit it was one of the more interesting of the occasional visiting experts we'd had over the weeks. Last week's visit by a hockey company rep was an exercise in selling new skaters all kinds of stuff. And there was the whole awkwardness about the fact he'd wanted to talk solely about the stick I had upstairs. I'd managed to get away by faking receiving a phone call and hiding in the kitchens.

Today was way more interesting. We had a hockey analytics expert visiting. He was going to show us cutting-edge techniques to improve our skating through numbers, and demonstrate we were more than goals and assists. My opinion, for what it was worth, was that a player learned skating when the blades hit the ice, and I wanted to see what the visitor had to say.

Also, Jacob was so excited, and it was a new hobby of mine to really like excited Jacob.

Hell, it was sexy to see Jacob *be* anything. Awake, asleep, eating, reading, I could look at him all day.

We had five days of our nine left, and after hearing from the analytics guy, we had a break and then team selection for the end of placement games. I hoped I was on the same team as Jacob, but it wasn't my call. I guess it didn't matter what team he was on. We won together, or he tried to defend against me, and I got past him and scored. Either way, it was win-win for me.

Over the past few days, we'd practiced a lot of kissing, and the hand jobs had been intense, to the point that I wanted more. Way more than just my hands on him, and I wondered every waking minute, when I wasn't in hockey mode just how far and fast we could take this sex thing before our time was up.

The only problem I had was that it wasn't just sex. Like take right now, for instance. I wanted to hold his hand on the way down the stairs to the lecture room. My hand itched with the need to touch, the lust for him all-consuming. I didn't touch him though, didn't even reach for him; we'd agreed we'd keep everything on the down low, or rather, that is what he'd said, and I'd gone along with it for his sake. It wasn't the man kissing man thing. He genuinely didn't care. No, it was more the Jacob kissing *Ryker* thing.

It seemed like anyone knowing he was exchanging messy, mutually satisfying hand jobs with Ryker Madsen was firmly on his *no* list. That was fine. We had five days left, and then we'd likely never see each other again. He wasn't going the NHL route, wanted to get back to his farm, and I was very firmly fixed on the NHL being my kind of forever.

When we reached the room, he joined his college friends, and for a second, I hovered until Scott swept in behind me, grabbing my arm and yanking me over to sit with the Eagles.

Much to mine, Lois's, James's and Will's horror, they were still all about pulling me into their little group, nurturing connections, and in their words, keeping like with like. I gave them a "what can you do" shrug, but God, it felt good not to have to sit with them. They weren't bad people at all, but they wanted something from me I wasn't willing to give—a way to underscore how important they were because of who their parents were.

That was how I ended up sitting two seats away from Jacob and wishing I could climb over the guys in the way and go to sleep on Jacob's broad muscled chest like a kitten. Ethan came in, and a tall, slim man with a clipboard and glasses followed. The new guy looked nervous, but boy was he gorgeous, if you liked your men brimming with understated sexiness. Ethan introduced him as Michael Campbell and spoke a little about what he was trying to achieve in this session.

Scott nudged me and whispered loudly. "Ask Jacob what he thinks of Mr. Sexy Stats Guy. Pass it on."

What were we? Teenagers? I instinctively glanced at Jacob who sat forward in his seat, a pen in one hand and his trusty notebook opened at a clean page. One day he'd turn a page and find where I'd drawn a penis halfway through, and I imagined the innocence I could feign that I would never defile his pages.

Because a penis in a clean notebook is always funny, dammit.

"Ask him," Scott urged.

"No," I whispered back. What Jacob thought of Michael Campbell wasn't something I wanted to find out.

Scott elbowed me again. "That's just his type. Seriously, ask Ben to ask Oscar to ask him."

I rounded on Scott. "No," I said simply, and I said it loud enough that everyone turned to look at me.

Scott's mouth dropped open, and his eyes widened, and he gave me the smuggest grin I'd ever seen. Then he reached around me to the big goalie and held out his hand. "You owe me ten, dude," he instructed Ben.

"You're screwing with me," Ben said.

Scott snorted a laugh. "Nope, told ya."

"Will you two give it a rest," I snapped under my breath.

"Excuse me, Mr. Saunders, Mr. Madsen, is there a problem?" Ethan asked pointedly.

I sunk in my seat and tried my best to appear innocent, glancing at Jacob and wincing when he returned my gaze and raised a single eyebrow in comment.

"No, Coach," I said, and Scott mumbled the same thing.

Actually, Michael, the stats guy, was kind of cool. He'd worked a lot with Boston and was currently working with the Rush AHL team, so he knew a lot about everything. I held back when the classroom emptied.

"Could I speak to you?" I asked him, aware that Jacob had stopped by the door and was waiting for me. I waved him away, and then it was just me and Michael left in the room. "I'm Ryker Ma—just Ryker."

We shook hands, and he smiled at me. "Just Ryker, it's nice to meet you. What can I do for you?"

"What if a team has issues that you can't prove with

numbers?" I blurted out, which was stupid because I had this long, complicated question all formed in my head. "Like, if it's obvious to everyone but them that they're messed up. What can a person do to prove what needs to change? If they get there and see problems, I mean." I finished lamely because I ran out of steam.

"Are we talking about your college team? You're with the Leicester Blades, right?"

"Yes, and no. I mean, yes, my college team, my coach, but I don't fit in there because... jeez, I don't know why. It's like I'm separate there, and I don't like it..." I stopped. That wasn't what I was there to talk about, and Michael had an expression that was suspiciously like sympathy. "Ignore that. This is about a hypothetical team."

He nodded as if he knew what was in my head, then closed the door and gestured for me to sit. When he sat opposite me, he waited for me to finish my question, and I double-checked that the door was shut and that the small room with the lines of chairs was empty. Hockey players didn't have doubts about where they ended up. They had lines they learned about working hard and taking opportunities.

He picked up I was struggling.

"Ryker Madsen, first round pick, Arizona Raptors."

"Yes."

"Do you have concerns over the team that drafted you?"

I looked back at the door, suddenly fearful that if someone heard him, they would tell the team and I'd be twisting in the wind, thrown from the program, canned by the Raptors.

"No," I said, then sighed. "It's not them, it's... I don't know." I felt like maybe I shouldn't be talking to anyone about this. Being a player is ninety percent bravado and hiding any kind of pain or worry, and I was clearly failing that.

"It's okay," he murmured and dropped his voice a little, which weirdly made me feel better. "I can certainly give you some statistical insight into a particular team, like Leicester, although my expertise isn't at the college level. But what you're asking here might well be less about numbers and more about the feel of the team. I always encourage teams to use the analytics to inform decisions, but always for them to be mindful of the character of a team. From the skaters themselves to the characteristics of coaching to the quality of the food in the kitchen, it all works. I know your stats; you have talent."

When he left, we shook hands, and I wasn't sure what to do next. There was so much information in my head, and I felt a little lost.

"Ryker? Is everything okay?" Ethan asked from the door to his office. Something in my face must have told him I was stressing because he stood to one side and gestured for me to go in.

"What's wrong?" he asked, and I took the chair opposite his desk.

"Did you see me play last season? In the lead up to combines and the draft."

"I caught a few games," he said, and was it just me or did he sound cautious?

"And?"

"What is it you're looking for, Ryker? You don't need me to tell you that you'll go far."

"I'm not sure whether to go back to college or if I should talk to the Raptors about a place on their AHL development team."

He sat back in his chair. "Okay, your dad is one of my

oldest friends, so I'm going to be super honest here. I would have expected more from you last season, so do you want my advice?"

No, I don't want to hear what I already know. "Yes."

"Don't focus solely on the numbers that show you are succeeding and being the best you can be. Look at your own playing, and check whether you feel as if you are playing to your best."

"I did feel I was. No, wait, I didn't, but it was okay because… no, it wasn't okay at all. Jeez, I'm not making any sense." I took a deep breath and settled my thoughts, and Ethan let me. "I came here, seeing the way the guys from the Eagles are here together, friends, you know, working to make each other better. We don't have that at Leicester. I know I could be a better player if I had coaches that cared about more than who my Dad is living with, or was on a team that was working with me instead of waiting for me to do it all." I hid my face in my hands. "Fuck, that was so arrogant."

"It's not arrogance to know your worth." Ethan paused awhile and then leaned forward. "Do you feel the team dynamic is wrong, or is the failure the coaching, or is it *you* that needs to change?"

"So, what if it is *me* that's the problem?"

He studied me intently. "I don't think I can help you with that, Ryker."

He shook my hand as I left, and as soon as I was out of the room, I headed for the tree by the lake. I knew Jacob would be there, head in a book, and I needed me some snuggle time. Had I held myself separate from my college team? Was it me who'd driven a wedge between the coaches and the team? I really needed a hug because when Jacob hugged me, I felt like nothing could hurt me and that I could make any decision I wanted.

Where did that come from?

"Hey, you done?" Jacob asked.

I snapped out of my daydream and realized I'd not only reached him but was staring at nothing. I shook my head to get rid of the mess and sprawled out next to him. "Yep."

"You've been in there a long time. Do you know that Michael guy?"

Was it just me or did Jacob sound odd?

"No, never met him before. Why?"

Jacob shrugged. "Thought he might be a friend of your dad's, and that was why you stayed behind."

I looked at Jacob, then narrowed my gaze when I thought I saw a flash of vulnerability in his expression. I could've been honest and explained my concerns about college. But that would've been exposing something of myself that I really didn't want to share just yet. Better that people thought I was happy, smiley Ryker without a care in the world than to see inside me to the insecurities below.

"You jealous?" I rolled onto my belly, propping my chin on my hands.

That got the response I wanted, and he poked at me with a foot. "Whatever. Now stop talking."

So I did. I lay there watching Jacob study, and wondering if there was a way to get him to stop reading just for some kissing. Luckily, my shaky masterplans didn't pan out as Scott and Ben both found us, and abruptly two became four.

"No, I don't want you all here," Jacob said as soon as they started to sit down. "Go away and take him with you." He pointed at me, and I rolled to my feet, pasting what I hoped was a cute and innocent expression on my face. He didn't glance up to see it, though, highlighting a passage in the book he was staring at and lost in his world of whatever the cows were doing in diagram one.

The three of us left him and walked back toward the center, and at the last minute, I slowed down. I imagined Ben and Scott would be doing something Eagles-wise and didn't want to be an extra.

"Wanna shoot some hoops, Mads?" Scott asked, already hustling toward the open area where there was a basketball court and everything set up for tennis.

"Me?"

Scott threw me a look that I couldn't decipher, then made a deliberate three-sixty. "I don't see anyone else around here called Mads."

Which was how I spent a while alternating shots with Ben and Scott, shooting the shit, and talking about the teams they'd choose if they ever made it to the NHL. Scott wanted to play for a Canadian team, *any Canadian team*, and he was quite explicit in that. He'd have preferred to play for his home city, Toronto, but he'd take the others as long as it was north of the border. Statistically unlikely, given none of us knew where we'd end up, but he hadn't gone through the draft like me this year, waiting to work his way through college. Ben, on the other hand, goalie extraordinaire, wanted to follow in Malcolm Subban's footsteps. In his words, he and Malcolm would make black goalies a thing to be scared of if you were shooting a puck at them. One day maybe I'd shoot on him, and it was never too soon to know that he was freaky good but had a weaker glove hand.

When we were done playing, the three of us sprawled on the grass for the remainder of the break.

"So tell me if what I heard about Ten is true," Scott began, and I tensed. "Ben here says he's the bastard love child of Gretzky and an alien."

"Cyborg," Ben amended. "It was Gretzky and a cyborg. A hockey-playing superhuman cyborg."

I relaxed at the bantering. "You'll never make me talk." Then I lowered my voice. "I will tell you one thing though. I did find him plugged into a wall socket once."

Ben snorted a laugh and shoved me. I shoved back, Scott sat on me, Ben tried to push my face in the grass, I managed to switch it so that I was sitting on Scott, and I knew one thing for sure. I'd made friends.

THEY PUT me on the opposite team to Jacob, and I made the best of it, thinking maybe I'd get some touching time without anyone realizing it.

Only I hadn't counted on that edge of speed he had now. The same speed that I had encouraged him to work on. He was also a brick wall, and I didn't have it easy. By the end of the fourth shift, when they put me up against him, I was having to work at getting past the big ox. At first, it was a rush of adrenaline that pushed me, and then it hit me as I was going over the boards on my next shift. I wasn't getting by and winning with fifty percent of my skill and speed. I was really having to actually *try*.

The guys with me were strong skaters, on a mission to win this game, which would be the first of three. Coach played with lines, pushed us to switch it up, had me playing center for some of it, and I felt strong in that position but more at home back on the wing. I was scrappy there, focused, fighting Jacob when he attempted to press me to the glass. I was smaller, faster, and even though I'd helped him work on his speed, I'd also seen the parts of his defense that I could break through. Every time I got past, I had to really freaking push myself, but I managed to get two shots past the goalie.

We won that first game by four goals to their two, and I owned the fact I'd contributed to my team. That meant something. Scott high-fived and whooped as we skated a stupid-ass victory lap, and I was exhilarated and on a natural high. When I hit a brick wall as I skated backward, I didn't even have to turn to know that Jacob was there behind me. I leaned into him briefly and then skated away.

I couldn't wait to get back to the room. With Jacob.

Scott and Ben commandeered us both after showers, something about beer or talking or god knows what. I wasn't listening to their back and forth after I'd said I needed to call home and Jacob said he needed to write up notes.

They didn't care. They weren't pushing us to do whatever social thing they had going on, but it was awkward when Scott tilted his head at Jacob and grinned at me.

"Have fun… uhm… studying and talking," he said and whistled as he walked away. *Ass.*

We made it all the way back to the room, all kinds of calm and collected. We even talked about the game and discussed strategies.

But when the door to our room was shut and locked, everything changed.

EIGHT

Jacob

WHAT *WAS IT* ABOUT THIS GUY?

Ryker Madsen was this wildly confusing, unanswerable riddle that left my brain spinning like tires on an icy road. There were times he annoyed the hell out of me. And then, like now, when he was standing in front of me, lids heavy with desire, lips wet and parted, hair flopping down into his eyes, that I wanted nothing more than to shove him onto the bed, peel him out of his clothes, and love him senseless.

"This is nuts," I mumbled yet still reached for him.

He came to me far too easily. I barely had to apply any pressure to have him melded to me, his hands up under the back of my shirt, and his tongue gliding over mine. This *was* nuts. It was insane. This could go nowhere. He'd go back home, and that would be it. It was stupid to keep pawing at each other like this, but I couldn't *not* touch him. Not when he looked at me through those thick lashes.

"This has got to be the last time, okay?" I panted between long, wet kisses that led us to his bed, our clothing coming off with sharp tugs that stressed seams until we were down to our underwear.

"Yep, last time. I promise." Ryker wore a mischievous smirk as he shoved me to the bed.

"You're lying."

He nodded, then crawled up over me, his teeth nipping a hot path along my belly to my chin, then back downward. "Get up here," he purred.

I slid my fingers into his hair, sighing as the silken strands slithered over my knuckles.

He wiggled free, my hand falling to my chest. I pushed up to rest on one elbow and then the other. Ryker sat between my splayed legs, his hands on my thighs, his gaze on my cock. "Would you be okay with me sucking you off?"

"Fuck, yes," I huffed, his query making me lightheaded.

A smile played on his lips, then disappeared when I tugged my briefs downward to free my dick. His eyes rounded a bit. I let him look. We'd never gone past a hand job or some grinding to get ourselves off. Simple stuff. Easy stuff. Stuff that meant nothing because every guy our age did it all the time with people they barely knew or even inanimate objects. I couldn't hazard a guess as to how many times I'd dry-humped the spare pillow on my bed back in my younger days. It was just to get off. Slake a drive, scratch that relentless itch. Meaningless. But this was more than a hump-and-spurt. This was far more intimate, and it rattled me as strongly as it enticed me. I could count on one hand the number of times I'd participated in oral sex. Four times. And three of those were terrible, toothy adventures with drunken guys at frat parties. There had been no homosexual encounters back home, aside from that infamous kiss. One questioning bisexual guy does not a vibrant love life make.

"I've never gone down on a guy before, but I'll be good." He bent over and took as much of my cock as he could get into his mouth. I gasped as he gagged. "Ack, oh, crap, sorry."

"It's cool." That was true. It was kind of nice seeing Ryker Madsen not knowing how to do something. There was no pro shop he could visit to buy the knowledge on how to suck dick. Watching him lap at the round head of my dick was hot. Spittle made his lips slick and deep pink as they slipped over my cockhead. He shimmied down a bit, getting his knees to the floor. I shifted downward, eager to have him suck on my head again. "Press on the underside of the head with your tongue. Yeah… shit, yeah."

His gaze rested on me as he tongued and licked, saliva eventually coating his fingers and my cock. I felt his teeth twice and had to remind him to be careful. Oh man, but the other sensations were amazing. I bucked up several times, trying to get myself deeper. He'd gag and pull off, then suck me back down. Ten times or so he did this, pulling on the head with his lips while working the shaft with his hand. Soft, contented noises rose from him.

"I'm close," I growled, giving him time to pull off. He didn't. Ryker took the load right on his tongue, swallowed, squeezed his eyes shut, and then scrambled into the bathroom to cough up a lung. I grabbed my dick and worked it hard, finishing myself off while he sputtered and made violently disgusting sounds. Cradling my balls, I curled in on myself, rasping and quaking until the tremors lessened and I could go check on him.

"Hey, you going to be okay?" I asked, peeking around the doorframe. He was lying over the sink, a bottle of blue antiseptic mouthwash in his hand, his cheek pressed tight to the edge of the big porcelain sink. "Did you puke?"

"Do not come in here," he rasped.

"Dude, really? We're going to get shy now? You just swallowed my spunk. I think we're past being bashful. Did you throw up?"

"No, it was close." He slowly stood, his rosy cheeks and sweaty brow plastered with long, brown tendrils of hair. His nose wrinkled. "I totally blew that, huh?"

"Well, yeah, you totally blew me."

He rolled his eyes, took another swig, gargled, and then turned to spit. "I feel like an ass."

I went to him, gathered him to me, and tucked his head under my chin. We kind of had to tip his head a bit to make it fit, but once we had things lined up, it was damn sweet.

"Not every dude can swallow," I told him, trying to sound as if I knew all about it when I didn't have a fucking clue. Sure, I read shit online, but practical application, like hot cum on the back of my throat? Nope, not a clue. "Or so I hear. I've never tried." He grunted in self-disgust as his arms tightened around my middle. "It's true. I've never fucked another guy either or had one fuck me."

He pulled back, his eyebrows knotted. "So you're a virgin?"

"Yeah, well, sort of. Yes." I sighed when he made a face. "I know you can't be sort of a virgin. I am, but, like, it's not that I haven't had offers." I paused, gauging how much of the truth I should tell this guy whom I would be saying goodbye forever to shortly. "Okay, that's not true. No one has ever asked. There was only one dude back home, and he wasn't exactly sure if he was into guys or not. Then when I got to Owatonna, there were lots of gay guys, but none that were interested in a big, hulking farm boy who reeks of barn. So, yeah, that's my story."

"I've been with two girls. No guys aside from kissing. But my hand has seen plenty of action."

That made me chuckle. Ryker did that a lot. Made me laugh, sometimes in frustration, but more and more frequently about something funny or cute he'd say or do. I placed my palm on his face and brushed back those sticky strands.

"Did you like it? With the girls?"

"Sure. I like girls. I like guys too. I like you a lot."

He wanted to be kissed, so I covered his mouth with mine, sweeping deeply into his minty-fresh mouth before I led him back to his bed. We tangled ourselves together, arms and legs knotting up, his chest tight to mine. I rolled him to his back, eager to get him off now. His dick was soft, but with a little oral persuasion, he was rock hard in seconds, and I had the pleasure of sucking him off with a touch more finesse than he'd shown. Nice to know there were a few things I did better than Ryker. When he came, I closed my eyes, letting the taste of him coat my mouth before swallowing. His nails dug deeply into my scalp, but I didn't pull off, even when my eyes watered. Nope. I sucked harder, pulling more hot grunts and low groans from the man until he was done thrusting and trembling.

I lapped at his cock then, cleaning off his perfectly curved dick. Our gazes locked.

"Show-off," Ryker said breathlessly.

I chuckled, kissed the head of his prick, and then wriggled into bed beside him, pulling him to my side, my right leg dangling off the mattress because we were that pressed for space.

"Someone needs to knock you down a peg or two, Madsen," I murmured into his thick hair, inhaling the subtle scent of his shampoo, a fresh lemony-citrus smell that I'd always associate with him. I drifted off then, his arm resting on my stomach, his hair tickling my nose. I slept like a baby that night.

. . .

THE LAST DAY AT CAMP, all the Eagles decided we had to do breakfast at this quaint little coffee shop in town. Why? I had no clue until Ryker and I shuffled in, the beautiful morning pretty dull for us despite the brilliant blue sky, the birds singing, and the puffy white clouds overhead. We had two hours left until we went our separate ways, and despite how I'd promised myself this little thing was just for sex, not waking up to hear him chattering away or see him spread out on his bed, hair all tangled from sleep or sex or both... it was going to suck.

Right, so enough about what was coming in two hours. The coffee shop had freshly baked muffins so big you needed two hands to hold them. Also, the staff was made up of cute girls in little green aprons who flirted with the team.

I flopped down next to Ben, who was attacking a blueberry muffin the size of a soccer ball, his eyes dropping shut in sheer bliss.

"I missed this kind of food." He sighed around his mouthful of empty calories. We'd done nothing but eat healthy for a month, and while that had shown up in a toned body and more energy, I could not deny that I was this close to drooling over the coffeecake muffin Ryker placed in front of me, along with a massive mug of hot coffee, black with sugar.

We ate, we talked, we made jokes, we drank coffee and said goodbye to the guys. Ryker shook the hand of every Eagle, promising to stay in touch, exchanging phone numbers and social media information. I waited on the sidewalk, hands in my front pockets, eyes on my old sneakers, for him to stop being so personable and well liked, but he never did stop being Ryker. And I kind of liked that about him. He pulled me out of myself, urged me to engage more. I was reclusive by nature, but with Ryker at my side, I had been more prone to stepping out now and again.

"I really like the guys on your team. They're very cool," he said after he'd made his last goodbyes and joined me for the walk back to the training facility.

"Yeah, they're the best." I was in no mood to talk. My gaze stayed on my feet as we rounded the lake, Ryker plodding along beside me, our elbows bumping on occasion. He stopped walking midway past the lake, making me peek up from my Keds to see what the problem was.

"I don't want to end this," he said it aloud, his face grave, his stunning eyes horribly sad. I threw a long look at the pair of mallards paddling past with several ducklings following behind.

"We said—"

"I know what we said, but I don't want to stop seeing you."

I let my eyes close for a second, and when I opened them, the lake was still there. Nothing had changed. Nothing was going to change.

"We said—"

Ryker scowled and threw a hand into the air. "I *know* what we said! Can you stop being so fucking *you* all the time and just feel something for once?"

"I feel shit!" I snapped right back. "But feelings aren't going to change the fact that you're in one world and I'm in another. I'm going back to Minnesota, to the farm, where I'll stay until fall term starts. There's probably second or third cutting hay waiting for me as we speak. That is my reality. Your reality is heading back to your fancy Ivy League school—"

"It's not Ivy League, and it's not some blueblood

academy. I thought we were past that stupid class shit!" Oh man, he was really mad now. His eyes sparked with ire, but I could see the pain mingled with the fire. Maybe fighting would be the best way to end this. Make him think I was a jerk who used him to get off and… and… shit. Those fucking eyes of his.

"We are past that. I'm sorry." I grabbed him up like a long-lost teddy bear and clasped him to my chest. He stumbled into the embrace, then wound his arms around me. "Default settings."

A duck quacked behind me, calling the babies maybe or just asking what was wrong with the two humans who were yelling at each other when the day was so glorious. Sometimes being a duck would've been so much easier.

"Ever wish you were a duck?" I asked, and he snorted into my neck.

"Daily, my man." He stepped back, his fingers still on my hips, his gaze now soft but still melancholy. "We'll keep in touch, yeah?"

"I'm not sure we should. That'll just make it hurt all the more, eh?" He mulled that over, frowning as he did, and then inclined his head in agreement. "Best to make the cut quick and deep. Sever it cleanly."

He kissed me, right there beside the pond, and I kissed him back, grabbing all of him that I could to last me through the withdrawal period that was about to start.

When we got back to Rayzor Edge, there were his father and Tennant Rowe, waiting for him. Ryker introduced me as his "good friend," and I shook the hands of two legends, then helped him pack his gear into the car that I'd so envied. Now I hated the fancy-ass SUV, but not for the same reason. I despised it now because it was taking him away and not because it was a status symbol. Maybe I *had* learned something after all…

Sitting in my old truck, Jake Owen's *The One That Got Away* rolling out of my phone, I swiped at my damp cheeks, then slammed it into drive. The healing arms of Minnesota farmland called.

NINE

Ryker
———

I DIDN'T USUALLY ASK DAD FOR A LOT OF FAVORS. WELL, not since I was old enough to understand the concept of making my own way in life. I didn't usually have to ask for his help because things happened naturally for me.

I wasn't stupid. I knew that my last name may have opened doors, and it wasn't as if I was *just* Ryker Madsen. I was Ryker Madsen, fourth generation skater, with a whole history of hockey in my family. Son of the famous Jared Madsen, the defenseman who'd been cut short in his prime, grandson of blah blah. You'd only have to listen to the radio during games I played in to hear the same thing over and over. Hockey was in my blood, or at least that is what the experts said every single time they mentioned me. Also, I was blessed with all kinds of cutting-edge gear, the best sticks, the finest skates, and I spent so much time with NHL teams over the years that many of the best players were unofficial uncles. Hell, I had a potential Hall of Famer as my godfather.

So no, I didn't really have to ask Dad for help. Until right now, when I wasn't able to use my name or who I knew to get something I thought I wanted.

But asking Dad a favor? That was causing me grief, and I'd yet to leave my room. My bags were packed to go back to Leicester, my books heavy, my heart heavier. I'd not had one text over the summer from the guys on my Leicester team, except for all the ones asking when it was Dad and Ten's day with the Stanley Cup and was there any chance they could see it. Yep, that was pretty much it, and it wasn't all their fault. I wasn't exactly putting myself out there to reconnect after the mess of last year.

That was just one more thing that told me Leicester was the wrong place for me. All I needed to do was go out there to Dad and ask for his advice, get him to pull some strings, and maybe I'd get to change the direction of my career, but more importantly, my life. He'd already called me out on my moping, and I told him I was antsy to get back to skating. Of course I was lying. What I really wanted was to be waking in the morning next to Jacob, his big hands holding me still, the taste of our kisses addictively hot.

You can't change your whole five-year plan because of a man.

But what if that man just happened to be playing for a college team that had a strong team ethic, cohesion, and also where I now had friends? Did that make what I wanted to do right?

Scott, Ben and I texted loads, sharing stupid memes, shooting the shit about trades and training camp. I didn't come out and actually ask them if Jacob talked about me, but after the fifth text asking casually in our chat group whether they'd heard from Jacob, Scott had lost it and called me to explain that yes, they texted, but no, they hadn't talked much past preparing for the new college year. It turned out they were getting a house off campus, which worked out cheaper all around, but they were tiny rooms.

Eight Owatonna U hockey players crammed into six rooms, some sharing.

I wanted to be there.

I think.

I hadn't received any texts from Jacob. Then again I hadn't texted him, and he didn't have an active ongoing presence on any of the social networks. He'd posted a photo of the summer camp to his Instagram, and it pretty much ended there.

"Ryker?" Dad knocked and called at the same time.

"Yeah?"

He opened the door cautiously and peered around it. What he would see was one miserable ass son who was worried about asking him for support.

"What's up?" I asked and sat upright in my chair.

Ten shoved Dad from behind, and he stumbled in, looking back at the door shutting him in the room.

"Jeez, Ten!" he shouted.

"Talk!" Ten bellowed back.

"Talk about what?" I asked.

"Ten says you have something to say to me, and apparently you are worried about it, and that I need to sit and listen before I lose my shit." Dad sat on the edge of my bed and huffed irritably. "That was a direct quote. So I'm here, and you need to know that whatever it is, I won't lose my shit, although if it's serious, then your mom might well lose her shit."

I couldn't help but tease him. He was so earnest.

"What if I'm going to be a daddy?" I asked and watched his mouth fall open. "I'm kidding."

"Asshole child," he snapped, then picked up the nearest thing to him, a Tennant Rowe bobblehead. He threw it at me, and I caught it easily and placed it down, giving myself extra time to think.

"I don't want to go back to Leicester." There, I'd said it, got the words out of my mouth and into the room where Dad could now officially lose his shit if he needed to.

Instead, he focused on me. "You want to leave college?" he asked patiently and leaned forward, his fingers laced and his elbows on his knees. "Do you want to talk to the Raptors, think about AHL? You know that comes with a whole shitfest of dangers if you're not ready."

"No, I don't need to speak to the Raptors, or at least, maybe I do, I don't know. Dad, I want to switch colleges."

I could see his expression turn from worried to shocked to concerned and then to confused.

"What college?"

I know he expected me to talk the big guns, like Wisconsin-Madison or Boston U, but that wasn't what I wanted or needed right now.

"Owatonna," I said and waited for a reaction. He nodded, so I forged ahead with my carefully thought-out plans. "Most of the team were at the summer camp, and they have a cohesion that Leicester doesn't have. It felt right to be with them, in a way that being at Leicester doesn't. They were interested in *me*, and I would work really hard at my hockey and my studying and be better for it. I have friends on the team, people I really want to work with, and they want to play with Ryker Madsen, not Jared Madsen's son." I let out a breath when I'd finished throwing all the words at him and waited for him to ask me questions or laugh at me. I didn't mention Jacob. I didn't need to, because he wasn't the entire reason I wanted to switch. Something different had to happen in my life.

Dad frowned. Not a good sign. "Okay, let's look at this

logically." He pressed a hand to his temple. "Would you even be able to switch at this late date? The Raptors would have to approve, and it's not like trading. You can't just up and go at a moment's notice."

This was the moment when I had to pull every string I could. "You know the Owatonna coach from your time at Buffalo, right?"

"Bob Quinton, yeah, I do—"

"And the Raptors would want the best NCAA development team for their first pick. Right?"

"Your agent will have something to add to this." Dad shook his head. "That is when it gets super complicated."

He blinked at me, and for the longest moment, I was in limbo, not sure what was going through Dad's mind. After a nod, he stood.

"And that's it?" he asked. "You don't have anything else on your mind?"

Jacob. Summer kisses.

"No, that's it."

Dad seemed relieved that I'd thrown something easy to help me with at him.

"I'll call him, but your agent is all on you, right?"

"I can handle Tommy," I said. Tommy was actually a nice guy and absolutely nothing to do with my grandpa, who'd brought in some complete sharks to talk to me. I'd found Tommy myself. He wasn't much older than Dad, and he truly wanted the best for me. What Dad didn't know is that I'd already spoken to Tommy with a lot of what-ifs. He was already behind me moving to Owatonna and said he'd work to get me there if the whole Dad thing didn't pan out.

I followed him to the door, and neither of us was surprised to see Ten waiting outside.

"What? Tell me," Ten demanded.

Dad muttered something under his breath and walked past Ten, who then looked at me expectantly. When I didn't immediately answer, he pushed me none too gently back into my room and shut the door.

"Out with it," Ten demanded. "What's wrong?"

"Nothing," I began, but Ten forged ahead.

"If it's an injury, we can handle that. I can pull a favor with the Railers PT and—"

"I'm fine, Ten, I just asked Dad to talk to a friend of his to get me late entrance into Owatonna."

"Owatonna, huh?" Ten immediately relaxed. We were close in age, and he could be like a big brother, but I'd decided he worried about me way too much and fit the *second dad* role very nicely. I loved Ten completely, loved the way he meshed into our lives and made Dad so damn happy. "Good school, solid team," Ten summarized, and I realized he was still talking.

"I know."

"Okay, I need to ask you something, and I want you to be completely honest with me because this is your future you're considering, and I need to know that…"

"What?"

"Are you messing with your future because of a boy?"

"I—what—no—what?" I managed in a wholly lame way.

"I knew it. Is this something to do with your *friend* Jacob?"

Ten wasn't teasing me or acting as if this was a joke. He was utterly and deadly serious. In fact, I don't think I'd ever seen Ten look so tense.

"No," I said immediately. I didn't think I was making the decision to change because of Jacob, but maybe in spite of him. I can't afford to be distracted right now, but Jacob took up a huge portion of my thinking time just the same.

"I'm not stupid, Ry. There was clearly a connection between you and him. Tell me you're not throwing your entire career path away for a guy you've met when you're only twenty?"

There were so many things wrong with that sentence, and I bristled immediately.

"One, you weren't much older when you met Dad, and two, this has nothing to do with Jacob and more to do with the Owatonna guys I met at camp, and three, Jacob is just a friend."

Ten got right up in my face, his green eyes sparking with emotion.

"One, I was already NHL when I met your dad. Two, this has everything to do with the friends you made, including Jacob, but mostly, three…" he crossed his arms over his chest. "Jeez, I can't remember three. I'm shit at this mentoring gig."

"Believe me, you're doing okay—"

"Wait, I have a three. Owatonna is a good school. I see a team there that is lacking a captain with skills, but it's a team that can go places, and if you want to develop, it's the place to be. But you need to remember you're not a journeyman who needs to work their way up. Just don't lose sight of what you want. Love, family, hockey, whatever you focus on, make it everything."

He backed away then with a shocked expression. "Fuck, I'm turning into my big brother."

Dad came into the room, waving his cell. "Quinton is ecstatic to consider the options, and he'll get back to me."

I hugged him then, and he held me tight.

"Do I need to remind you that you should be doing this for all the right reasons?" he asked. "Or did Ten channel big brother Brady and tell you already."

Ten joined in the hug, making it a three-way kind of thing.

"I used my best Brady voice and already told him." Ten sounded equally smug, then horrified with himself.

"God help us all," Dad muttered.

OWATONNA IS one of those old universities that used to be private and monied, but that had now been infiltrated by the masses, who called the old stone buildings their academic home. It was a campus of over two thousand. Lots of red brick buildings and stately oaks.

Dad and Ten helped me to move in. Ten was attempting incognito again, pulling the brim of his cap down farther, which meant he couldn't see where he was going. He barreled into Dad, causing him to drop the box he was holding, which led to Ten being more the center of attention than he would've if he'd left the cap off entirely. Not that everyone there was a hockey fan, but this was a Minnesota institution, and the percentage of people who knew hockey, and therefore Ten had to be high.

Somehow, after he'd signed a few autographs, we made it to my dorm room. A big space, brand new, that I, at least, didn't have to share with anyone. It came with the added benefit of a small bathroom with a toilet built into the corner, and a bigger than average bed. It wasn't quite as nice as Rayzor's, and of course it didn't come with a second bed holding a sexy farmer, but still, it was good.

All going well, maybe next year, I could share with the team.

"I'm worried," Ten announced as he peered into the bathroom.

"What about?" Dad latched onto Ten's worries because that is what dads did best. Worried.

"The bathroom is tiny, Ry." He looked at me in all seriousness. "Where will you fit all your hair products?"

"Ha fricking ha." I shook my head in disappointment. "Low blow, Rowe," I singsonged.

By the time Dad and Ten had left, I had all my hair products in a neat row on the small shelf. Of course there wasn't room for things like toothpaste, and I decided that would have to sit in the sink for a while until I thought it through. I peered into the mirror and pulled on one of the errant curls that fell onto my forehead. Maybe it was time for the flow to get cut back. If I wanted to be a serious hockey player and study, maybe I needed to spend less time on looking my best until I actually made it to the NHL for real.

Then again, Jacob loved my hair. He loved to play with the curls, and hell, I loved it when he wound it around his fingers. Also, this was some cool hockey flow, despite the regular trims and conditioning treatments.

Then it hit me. I was standing in my room staring at myself, rating my hair on a one-to-ten scale, and this was just freaking pathetic. I had things to check out. The rink, the training facility, all the things I wanted to discover on my own, much to Dad's disgust because he'd wanted to get in there and check it all out with me. Selfishly, I wanted to experience it by myself, and grabbing my key and my cell, I set off to find out what Owatonna U was all about. Unlike some of the other big-name colleges, the rink was on campus. Admittedly, it was on the very outside edge and was also available for public skates, but it was close enough to walk to from the dorms, and from the outside, it looked good. The building it was housed in was new. I'd read up on it, and it'd been built only six years ago. Glass, steel, and concrete, it included an amazing rink. Never let it be said that Owatonna U didn't invest in sports.

I could see the main concourse through the glass, and this late in the afternoon, it appeared to be empty. I guessed practice sessions had finished for the day, and it was before evening workouts and skates. Signs indicated that public skate was available at certain times, but that wasn't until tomorrow. I headed straight for security. Who knew if they'd even let me inside, but maybe I could just find a vantage point through a window to see the ice. I didn't have to do the whole thing.

"Ryker?"

I recognized Scott's voice immediately and spun to face him. He was weighed down with equipment bags and wore the gold and brown of Owatonna's hockey team. "Jesus," he said and dropped the bags. "What are you doing here?"

"It's a long story," I said and held up a fist to bump. He didn't leave me hanging and then pulled me in for a sideways bro hug.

"You never told me you were coming," Scott said and glanced behind him. I could hear the raised voices of an approaching group. "No one said you were coming."

"It was last minute."

"You didn't tell anyone?"

I knew what he meant. Had I really not said anything to Jacob?

I didn't have a chance to answer him. I spotted Jacob before he saw me. He was deep in conversation with Ben, his rucksack over one shoulder, the one I knew would be full of books, and his equipment in the other. He was the tallest on this team, and when he saw me over everyone else's heads, he stopped dead still. The rest of the team parted around him, some grumbling good-naturedly. Then the ones I recognized from the summer came over and fist-bumped, asked me what I was doing there.

"I transferred," I murmured. I didn't want Jacob to hear that thrown so casually out. Coming here might seem odd, as if I was chasing him down or something, and we'd said we were done.

Stalker alert.

"You coming down now?" Scott asked, and when I didn't answer, he must have gotten the hint. He encouraged the rest of the team away from me. Everyone fell silent, but Jacob hadn't moved. He didn't seem to be pissed, but maybe he was acting really well because he didn't look happy. He actually looked like a startled animal caught in the headlights.

"Jacob." I took a step closer.

"What are you doing here?"

"I transferred."

"From Leicester."

"Yep."

"To here?"

"Yes, to Owatonna."

In a flurry of motion, he was right up in my space, and because I didn't move away, I found myself in the position of having to crane my neck to look up at him, right into stormy blue eyes.

"Why?"

"There are a lot of reasons why." I stepped back a little, just a short way. "The program for business is good here, the team is here, but mostly I have friends here." I didn't mention that he had factored into my decision at all. Because in my head he was just a welcome thing on the list. Hockey was the main priority and would always be.

He closed down then, right in front of me, his eyes shuttered, his expression wary.

"I play hockey," he began. "I work two part-time jobs. I study. I don't have time to mess around with someone who has money and doesn't have to work as hard as I do."

He brushed past me, the book bag connecting with my hip, and fuck, it was heavy.

"I thought you knew me, that you'd seen past that," I said urgently.

He rounded on me then, bags flying, his eyes narrowed. "Don't mess with my life, Ryker. It may not seem like much to you, but I'm surviving just fine, and I don't have space in my head for any more."

"Jacob." I held out a hand to touch him, even though he was too far away. Maybe I hoped he would hold my hand or admit he was pleased I was here. He did neither. Then he turned his back to me and strode after the team. I followed immediately, slipping through the closing security door watching Jacob walk away.

I'd be happy to stay away from him, just play hockey on this team, and never kiss him again. I hadn't come to Owatonna *just* for him. I had friends for the first time, real friends like Scott and Ben. The team was excellent here, one of the NCAA's finest up-and-coming teams. This was a good place for me. It wasn't all about Jacob.

I rubbed my chest right over my heart because hell, I was lying to myself. If I hadn't come here hoping Jacob would be pleased to see me, then why did his dismissal hurt so much?

TEN

Jacob

"... FIRST ASSIGNMENT WILL BE ACCESSING THE WEBSITES OF all governmental agencies that impact the food system in the United States. Those include but are not limited to the U.S. Department of Agriculture and the Food and Drug Administration. You are to collect important information from each of the websites you visit, citing what roles these agencies play, the types of foods they oversee, and the range of information available via their websites. I'm sure, after you visit your chosen sites, and I will accept no less than ten, that you will have a better understanding of these agencies and how they impact farming operations. Use five sentences or less. Verbosity will be penalized. I want succinct answers. Turn in your work tomorrow by eight a.m. via our OU Blackboard site. Please note my serious face as I say that I brook no stupid reasons for not completing assignments. This is not a petting zoo class. Physiochemical and Biological Aspects of Food is an advanced class in our ag study curriculum. I expect excellence from all of you. In fact, I demand it. If I see less than excellence, I will fail you. Good day."

We all sat there, faces slack, staring blankly at Professor Gillard—a short man who reminded me of Professor Flitwick but was much meaner—before he waved us out of his classroom with a flick of his hand.

"Fuck, that dude is a charmer," someone muttered behind me as we filed out.

"I think I want to change my major," someone else complained.

"Anyone know where that petting zoo class meets? I feel the need to hug a sheep," yet another student asked as we made our way outdoors.

I didn't know their names. Just guys and girls who loved farming as much as I did. Who had time to make friends? Or socialize? Or start up again with the guy I'd had a thing with over the summer? Why was Ryker even there? How did he manage to transfer and why? *Why is he here?*

I jogged through Gladys Peterson Park—or GP Park as the students call it—a small but heavily used area of trees and benches, not seeing the students sitting around sipping coffee while they hung out with friends. Who had time for that? I had to be at the library in five minutes, pull four hours there, and then head off campus for my job at Pepper's Pizza Parlor for the eight-to-midnight shift. Then home, sleep, morning skate, classes, repeat until Christmas break. I really needed someone to remind me of how much fun college was supposed to be because, honestly, I wasn't seeing all the fun.

There was no time for Ryker, his hair, his smile, his strong body all hot and pliant under mine, or his taste on my tongue. I'd purged him after we'd left Canada. It had taken me weeks, but I'd finally gotten him out of my system. Or so I'd thought. Then he showed up here, among my team, on my campus, and I had to admit to myself that I'd not expunged him at all. Nope, he was still there, nestled nicely around my heart like one of those crocheted cozies my grandmother made for coffee mugs. Ryker was like that. A soft, woolen cozy that cradled my icy cold heart. And that sucked because I had no clue on how to deal with him residing there.

Why is he here?! How was I supposed to juggle everything and him? I paused, looked around, and realized I was down by the football field that sat next to the hockey rink, which was where Ryker and some of the Eagles would be now, playing around on the ice, honing their skills, growing closer, bonding. Yeah, great, so my stupid mind and feet had carried me there instead of the fucking library, which was in the opposite direction of the rink.

"Fuck this year already," I snarled, turned, and ran full bore to the library.

FOUR DAYS LATER, I was standing on the ice, surrounded by my teammates, getting this longwinded speech about cohesion and something else that started with a C. Confusion? Constipation? Commitment? Yeah, it was commitment. Coach Quinton wanted us to be one hundred percent committed to hockey, or else we could leave the ice now. He demanded commitment from every one of us, just like every professor, parent, and employer I'd had. But it was kind of hard to be one hundred percent committed to everything all at once, wasn't it? I glanced to the left, and there he stood, among the forwards, his eyes bright and focused, his hair hanging out from under his helmet. Ryker Madsen was the prettiest man I had ever seen. I wanted him so badly I ached inside, as though my soul was bruised or something.

"Benson, you want to repeat what I just said?"

My sight flew from Ryker to our head coach. I stammered and stuttered. Finally, he held up a hand, and I fell silent.

"The next time I ask a question of this team, I expect a concise answer."

"Sorry, Coach," I mumbled around my mouthguard. Everyone gave me that pitying look, including Ryker, which only made me feel more pathetic and overwhelmed.

"Let's get this scrimmage going." Coach glowered at me, then skated to the home bench. Today, we were playing against each other, brown jerseys against gold. We'd had two weeks to practice and start to find our footing as a team. Our first game was in ten days against Grand Forks U, one of our NCHC rivals. Thankfully, we didn't play the number of games the pros did. Our schedule was sixteen games with a five week break at Christmas. Praise Jesus. If we'd tried to keep an NHL-like schedule of eighty-some games a season, none of us would've graduated. I was having doubts about seeing a passing GPA for my sophomore year as it was, without hockey. I fought back a yawn, then skated out to center ice to stand to the left of Zach, my usual defensive partner.

"You look like shit."

I threw Zach a bored look.

"Wait until midterms, then call me ugly," I replied.

"I feel that," Zach grunted.

The puck was dropped by one of the assistant coaches. I glided back as the puck rolled to Ryker. He spun, puck on his stick, his gaze meeting mine, and a flash of awareness marked his expression. Without warning, he passed me. I knew that was my fault. I was supposed to read the subtle signs of the puck carrier and know before he did which direction he was going to go. He was now well around me and gunning for Ben, who just happened to be fucking amazing and kicked away the prime shot on goal.

I bit down on my mouthguard, glowered at the ice, and pushed my way into the small group of guys behind the net battling for the puck. I might not have been as fast as Ryker Madsen, but I was bigger. Considerably so. Using that bulk, I drove my shoulder into Ryker's back, hard, flattening him to the glass and then pushing all my weight into his spine so he couldn't move. Then for added measure and because he was wiggling free, I hooked an arm around him, enjoying the squirming mass of hard male against me for just a second before several whistles blew.

"Fucking stop holding me!" Ryker barked, shoving back at me, using his elbow and stick to break the bear hug I had him in. I shoved him into the boards. He spun around and took a swing. I gave him a solid push, two-handed, that flung him into the glass so hard the see-through panels shook as if we were having an earthquake. Ryker got madder, which was fine with me because I was mad at him too. He made a lunge at me which was only stopped by several of our teammates. Zach and Ben were there, pulling on me, jerking me from Ryker who was panting and cussing and flinging nasty words in my general direction as Scotty and John held him back.

"Benson, I want you in the showers *now*." I blinked away the sweat in my eyes. Coach Quinton was right there, in my face, and he was not amused. "Madsen. You too. Both of you are done here for the day."

Ryker skated past me, his helmet in his hand, long hair plastered to his head, eyebrows so deeply drawn you could barely see his irate gaze.

We made it as far as the locker room before he turned on me. I wasn't scared of him, not really, but he did make me aware that he was all man and he was pissed.

"This is bullshit!" He threw his helmet across the dressing room, his gaze never leaving mine. "I don't know what your issue with me is, but this shit on the ice is *not* going to happen. If you cost me a spot on this team, I will kick your ass! I've worked too hard to get where I am to let some stupid asshole like you derail my goals!"

"You took a swing at me. I didn't try to hit you." I stated that calmly and coolly, then went to walk around him.

He spun me to face him. The man was beautiful in his anger. His face was flushed, and his pupils blown. He looked nearly as good angry as he did when he was lost in passion.

"You were blatantly holding me. That's fucking horseshit in a scrimmage game. I know you hate me again, but this is not going to happen on the ice. You hear me?!"

He poked my chest, and yeah, I felt it. I exhaled, trying to let some of the gnarled-up toxins inside of me out, but they stayed put.

"Jacob, I mean it. If you don't want to be with me as we were in the summer, fine. I get that. We had our fun and all." A spark of pain came to life in his gaze, which made me feel even shittier because... just because. Had he come here thinking we'd be together again? Why? Why would he think that, and why did I want that so damn bad? "Hockey is my life. It's not just a game I'm playing to pay my way, so do not fuck this up for me, okay?"

I nodded. He was right. My shit was going to get us both benched. If I didn't play, I didn't get money, simple as that.

"Okay, yeah, I won't let our shit spill out on the ice again."

"Good. Now fuck off." He stalked past me to his cubicle. I stood rooted to the spot, unable to look away from him whipping his pads into his stall. When he looked at me, I glanced away in shame and went to my space, far from him, and began undressing, our eyes never meeting again that day.

LIVING in a house with seven other hockey players was a clusterfuck most days. Thankfully, I roomed with Ben, who was probably one of the quietest and tidiest people I had ever come across, especially in the mornings. Not that I slept late, even on weekends. My internal clock woke me no later than 5 a.m. no matter the day or where I was. So the fact that it was a Saturday and there were no classes meant nothing. I was awake. And Ben was sitting on the floor at the foot of his bed, on a yoga mat, in nothing but soft gray shorts, his eyes closed, his breathing slow and steady, his wide shoulders sloped with relaxation.

"Morning," Ben said, never turning to look at me.

"How'd you know I was awake?" I lay there staring at the ceiling, not moving a muscle save for my eyelids.

"As soon as you wake up your breathing accelerates."

"Is that bad?"

"I don't know, is it? Seems like you'd have a few minutes of calm before you start piling on the stresses."

I rolled to my side, eager to see something aside from one of my best friends giving me that look. It was the look I always got from the few people I called friends. A combination of worry and sadness, as if my life was so horrid they were this close to an intervention. Yeah, life did kind of suck, but the weak needed to be culled. Just as back on the farm. That was a lesson we country boys learned early.

"I have to go to work in an hour to open the pizza shop. Should I be Mr. Zen about that?" I asked the poster of Malcolm Subban that looked down upon us. I had no shit on the walls because what would I hang up? A poster of a hot Holstein? So Ben filled the walls with hockey and bands and corkboards with assignments and game schedules.

"Why don't you try some meditation with me?"

"Yeah, nope, thanks." I kicked off the covers, sat up, rolled my shoulders and neck, and then padded around the man on the purple mat.

"I think you should try to center yourself before you go downstairs," Ben said, his soft brown eyes on me.

I tugged up my shorts, shook my head, and left our room. Our house had two stories, six bedrooms, and one bath upstairs, kitchen and living room downstairs. Yeah, eight dudes and one bathroom. As soon as I stepped out of our room, which was immaculate, I could smell two things: hockey pads and stale beer. Three, if you counted the coffee someone had made, but the rank odor of pads and beer kind of choked that out. As soon as I reached the living room— which was covered with pizza boxes, beer bottles, and something that I tripped over which turned out to be a woman's purse—I flung open a window, untangled my foot from a purse strap while wondering which bedroom the purse-owner was in, and turned on a light. There sat Ryker Madsen on our beat-up sofa, holding a mug of coffee. He looked like a hare who had thought himself safe until the fox fell into his burrow.

"What are you doing here?" I asked as soon as the shock wore off. I let go of the bright pink purse.

Ryker's eyes moved over me, lingering for a bit on my upper chest before they darted to the window I had just opened, his cheeks a light pink that turned me right the hell on.

"I'm meeting Scott and Ben for some early ice time. They're uh—not up yet. They said to make myself at home, so I made more coffee. Ben said it was okay to wait down here."

"Oh."

And on that note, I went back to my room because my cock was getting hard, and I did not want Ryker to see that he still had that kind of effect on me. Ben cracked an eye when I slammed the door behind me. I frowned, inhaled the soft aroma of lemon-scented furniture polish, and sat in front of him on the cool wooden floor.

"Ryker was downstairs," I whispered, shoving at my dick after he closed that one open eye of his.

"I tried to tell you to center yourself, but did you listen?" The corners of his mouth tugged up into a soft smile. Then he opened both eyes. They were really nice, framed with thick lashes. I liked the warm brown color. "What's the deal with you two?"

"Can we just do yoga stuff?"

"You *really* want to try yoga and meditation?"

"Sure, why not?" I couldn't go back downstairs, and I was not about to jump into a Ryker/Jacob discussion at ten minutes after five. "I can do ten minutes to center, then go to work for eight hours, then come home and do more on that paper for Farm Implements and Engine Theory for Monday."

Ben studied me for a long time. I looked down and tried to get my legs into a lotus with the grace and ease he was seated in. Bendy goalies are not natural.

"I'm not sure ten minutes of meditation will help your killer stress levels much, but it sure won't hurt. Also," he added before I gave up on the cross-legged stuff and just let my long legs rest in front of me, "if you'd talk to me about things, maybe it would help."

I crinkled my nose.

"Right, well, no man is an island as they say. Close your

eyes. Breathe in and breathe out."

"My leg will not go behind my head, just throwing that out there."

Ben chuckled softly. "You're fine, man. We'll just see if we can loosen the knots your neck and shoulders are in."

I reached up to feel my shoulders. Yeah, they were tight, but what else was new?

"So breathe in and out and get rid of the voices chattering in your head."

I did as told, taking deep breaths. The voices were hard to get rid of. I opened an eye to check the clock on the nightstand. Ben caught me.

"I have to be at work in thirty minutes," I meekly stated.

"You have to get rid of all that monkey chatter inside your head." He tapped his temple, then tipped his head. "Can you do that?"

"Obviously not. I just failed yoga."

"No one fails yoga. Yoga is a journey. Okay, try thinking, 'I'm breathing in, I'm breathing out' with each breath. That gives you something to focus on."

"I'm focused on the fact that I'm going to be late to work and get fired. Then I'll be poor and unable to eat," I replied, shoving to my feet. "Thanks though. I feel loads better."

"You know what just might make you feel even better?" Ben gazed up at me.

I shrugged, then went to my dresser to find some clean clothes, but they were few and far between. I needed to do laundry today too. Miserable to-do list never got any shorter.

"A raging bender?" I said as I dug for clean socks and found two that didn't match.

"Ah *no,* talking to Ryker and working out this twisted romance the two of you are caught up in."

I glanced over my shoulder, one black sock and one white

sock in hand. "I have no idea what you're talking about. Go back to meditating and doing dog poses, dude."

"Mm-hmm, whatever. I'm just saying that if I had a man who looked like Ryker and was obviously as hot for me as he is for you, I'd be acting on that."

I had to turn around to gape at him. "Uh, since when are you into dudes?"

"I've always been into just about anyone. I just don't broadcast it. I like my guys a little older, is all."

"Ah, well, okay. I'll for sure meditate on all of that while I scrub pots and mop the floor."

I opted to go without socks that day. As hard as I tried not to spend my eight-hour shift mulling over the blisters on my heels or Ryker, I found myself wondering if maybe Ben had a point about Ryker, me, and the twisted mess that had been, at one time, a beautiful romance about to burst into bloom. Fighting the attraction wasn't working;. If anything, it was grinding me even deeper into the ground. I still wanted him. I'd never *stopped* wanting him. He brought light and energy and laughter to my life, and those were good things. Things that every living thing needed. Things that *I* needed to survive this world that just kept piling more and more weight on me.

I spent hours staring at soap bubbles and seeing Ryker's face in the foam. Perhaps if I cultivated this withered relationship with Ryker, I'd have someone to help carry the burdens. Oh man, and someone to make me smile again would be super fucking nice. Maybe we could at least be friends if nothing else, since I'd probably killed any chance for something deeper.

Maybe instead of trying to choke it out like a weed, I should give it a little sun and some fertilizer… I mean, I *was* a farmer after all. If I couldn't make good feelings grow, then who could?

ELEVEN

Ryker

I HADN'T MEANT TO STAY THE ENTIRE NIGHT. SCOTT AND I shared an economics course, and neither of us could get our heads around game theory or the Nash Equilibrium. This necessitated both of us sitting in Scott's room to study, but actually all we did was stare at each other blankly for a good half hour before we gave in, got beers, and pulled out the Xbox. When ten became eleven and I was falling asleep, Scott left me where I was, and that was it, I was gone. At least there was no bowl of cereal for me to fall into this time.

When Scott shook me awake at ass o'clock, he did it with coffee to hand, and we'd decided to get some early ice time in. So I waited around. If only I'd gone, then I would never have seen Jacob, all sleep-mussed and sexy.

Which was the image I carried with me all freaking day. After our fight at the rink, I thought we could at least be civil with each other, maybe even exchange more words.

All he'd done was ask me what I was doing there, and that was pretty much it. There wasn't even a smile or any talk of reconciliation or a pause for me to say something. Not that I would even have known what to say.

Where is my smile, my way with words? Where did my confidence and ability to get up in people's faces go?

I never even got the chance to ask if he wanted to join Ben, Scott, and me for early ice time. Would I have, even if I'd had the time? I had the chance to call after him or follow him upstairs. Scott was up there, and he was my friend. Ben was up there doing yoga, or so Scott said . He wouldn't have minded me stretching with him.

I didn't do either.

Jacob had made it perfectly clear that the summer had just been about getting off, and that even though he said he'd seen the real me, he actually had no idea of the person behind the labels I carried around.

"What's up?" Scott slid into the chair facing me, his tray of food consisting of carbs with a side order of more carbs. The protein on the plate was suspiciously chicken-like, but not enough that he'd chosen it himself. My plate was all pasta because they couldn't mess that up, right?

"Nothing," I lied.

Scott rolled his eyes but didn't add any words, shoveling the first mouthful of pasta and chewing with a thoughtful expression. He swallowed, then moved on to questions immediately.

"So you and Jacob. Spill."

I knew this interrogation would happen at some point. I could tell that he and Ben were desperate to ask me this morning. I'd even seen them shoving each other and looking my way. Neither of them manned up though, so I got away without having to think about what to say.

"Nothing." That was my go-to answer today.

"What the hell happened between you two?"

"Nothing."

"No, don't give me that 'nothing' shit. What changed from camp to now?"

I shrugged. I needed an entire afternoon to explain everything that was wrong between me and Jacob. I was still angry with him over what'd happened in the rink and the fact he'd blown me off this morning. I hadn't started that shit in the rink, and if Coach hadn't intervened, just how far would it have gone? Jacob had said he could leave our shit off the ice, but what did that even mean? And why didn't he want to talk now?

But mostly, why the hell had he pushed me into the boards and held me there? All I'd done was acknowledge him as we started the scrimmage, and suddenly he'd been on me like a fly on shit. Nothing warranted him getting up in my grill. And what if he'd hurt me? He'd held me and pushed me with intent, and that shit was not on.

But.

It was me, wasn't it? All my fault. I was the one who'd come to his university, pushing my way into his space, pulling a favor through my Dad, being the spoiled son he thought I was. I'd just reinforced all the stereotypes.

"Ryker? Dude? You okay?"

Scott poked my arm, pulling me out of my thoughts.

I shook off his hold. "I'm good."

"You don't look it."

That anger I felt with Jacob poked at me again, and it laced my voice. "Leave it, Scott."

"Ry—"

"Not everyone wants to talk out their feelings."

I snapped the words, and I don't know what I was expecting from Scott. Maybe for him to tell me to get bent or worse. I held a hand up to stop him before he could speak.

"Sorry," I apologized.

Scott raised a single eyebrow in silent condemnation, forked up another load of pasta, and chewed it, all the time looking at me. Then he put his cutlery down and sighed.

"Dude, seriously, have you tried talking to him? I've known him a year now, and he's a good guy. He works twice as hard as everyone because, I guess, he wants to fulfill his dreams the same as you do." He blinked at me as if he couldn't believe he'd used the words fulfill and dreams in the same sentence. Then he rubbed his chest. "Sometimes I scare myself," he muttered, then thumped me. Hard.

"What the hell?" I asked and shoved him back.

"Ask him what the fuck, and then talk the fuck back, and then..." he stopped and wrinkled his nose. "Maybe, fuck?"

Ben joined us then, and the talk turned to the fact that Ben had an essay to write on the ethics of authenticity and he didn't even understand the question, let alone have any idea of an answer. Not that I could help at all. By the time we'd finished eating, my chest was tight, and my need to talk to Jacob was making it hard to concentrate on anything else. I just had to track him down.

The start of my statistics class clashed with his Environmental Policy class. His break was right in the middle of my economics group, and at that point, it had been three hours since I'd decided I wanted to find him. We were due at the rink for practice at six, and that didn't leave much time to talk, but if I could just get everything off my chest, then maybe we wouldn't end up scrapping on the ice because of all my pent-up tension.

I blamed Scott completely. He'd made it all sound so simple. Talk to Jacob, establish where we stood, find out what he really thought, and then fuck. The way he said it had sounded so damn easy, but when I finally found Jacob, I was lost for words. He'd found another tree, one on the edge of the campus in GP Park, a wide oak tree that gave him shade and a quiet peaceful place to sit. Soon all the leaves would turn for fall and then drop, but right now, the ground was compacted earth and grass. He was completely focused on the book in his lap, his big body hunched over it.

I couldn't breathe, and I took a few steps back, instinctively moving away. I wanted to know why we'd fought, what he thought about me, about us, but what if he sent me away with a final no to even being friends? I didn't want the end of things to happen right here and now. I took another step back.

"What do you want?" he asked, looking right at me.

I didn't move fast enough.

"Just to talk. Scott said I should talk to you, to ask you…"

"Scott said."

He sounded disappointed, and I felt like a complete loser. This wasn't me. I could talk to anyone. I wasn't shy or unsure of my place in the world normally. But with Jacob I felt lost. *Stupid.*

"Can I?" I asked and gestured to the space next to him. He didn't drop his gaze, and then he sighed and shut his book.

"I guess," was all he offered, but he sounded more than uncertain. Even so, I moved there quicker than I thought possible, sitting facing him and crossing my legs at the knees.

"What did I do?" I asked the one question that burned. "Because coming to Owatonna was about making me a better player, and I know I should have warned you, but when we said goodbye, it really was *goodbye.* I want to make this place work, but I hate that you're angry with me."

"I'm not angry." He chose his words carefully, and the more he said the more rehearsed his words sounded. "Whatever we had in the summer had an expiration date, and you come back into my life and expect us to carry on. Like you don't understand I can't do this."

I wanted to say I didn't expect to carry on, but I couldn't lie. If we were going to salvage any kind of friendship from this, then I needed to be honest and direct.

"Yes, part of me was hoping you'd be interested in something with me, but the reason I came here was more that I saw what you had with your team, your friends. With Scott and Ben and how everyone accepted you for who you were. I wanted some of that. I was jealous."

"So you want to take what I have?" Jacob finally offered.

That wasn't the reaction I'd been expecting. Shouldn't he be saying something like I had nothing to be jealous about, that actually he had room in his life and with his friends for there to be more people?

"No, I don't want to take anything from you," I defended. "I just wanted to play and learn and work hard at my career and be near my new friends and you."

"This is all your fault," he said, his voice even. He didn't even sound as if he was accusing me; more that it was him accepting this solution.

"What? Why is it my fault?"

He crossed his legs the same as me. "I'm angry with myself because you made me think I could have someone like you, someone as strong and talented and focused as Ryker Madsen. But I can't, okay. I have a farm to save, a future I passionately believe in as much as you believe in hockey, and there is no room in it for you."

There were so many things in that speech that I took issue with, but I realized it didn't answer my question. "I still don't get how it is my fault."

He curled his hands into fists.

"Because I see you, and you're everything I didn't know I

needed. I want you, and if I give in, it will destroy everything I'm working for."

"Jacob—"

"No, you don't get it. I work two jobs. I'm trying to get this degree to help save my farm. The only reason I can stay here is that I get the financial help, combined with the hockey scholarship. It's all so finely balanced. If I had you as well, one of those things would slip. So which one do I give up, Ryker, huh?"

I knew I had to see his situation from his side.

"Friends then? Can we do that?"

He closed his eyes briefly, and when he opened them, they were bright with emotion. "No, Ryker, we can't be friends."

My heart sank, and I nodded. I could be an adult about this and understand what was happening here, even if my gut was twisting into a tight knot.

"I'm sorry I don't have to work to pay my way. I'm sorry I don't need a scholarship. I'm sorry I'm Ryker Madsen."

Man, I wanted to punch him. Or cry. Maybe both. I stood and brushed at the seat of my jeans.

He looked up at me and shook his head slowly. "I'll never be sorry you're Ryker Madsen," he murmured.

There was a little spark of hope there. "Can we at least not be enemies?" I asked in a small voice.

He nodded, and I left.

I made it all the way back to my dorm, with its private bath and its huge bed and the collection of hockey sticks that Ten and Dad had given me, and I closed the door, then locked it very deliberately.

Hands shaking, I pulled out my cell phone, thumbed my contacts, and sat on my bed. I spoke before Mom could even say hello.

"Mom, I don't know what to do, with me, with school, with hockey, with everything. I need your help. It's a guy, and I think I'm falling for him, and I think he hates that I don't have to pay my way through college or have a job. He says he doesn't hate me for that, that he's not angry with me, but he says we can't even be friends. I can't believe I'm calling you. This is so stupid."

I realized that was a hell of a lot of information to dump on her, but she was my Mom. She could handle everything I threw at her.

"Start from the beginning," she said.

So I did.

OLIVER PEMBERTON WAS a fussy librarian sort, which kind of fit with the fact he ran one of the three bookshops on the Owatonna campus. His was the shop that dealt with secondhand books, and his shop was like something out of *Harry Potter*. Shelves were filled haphazardly with everything from childcare to astrophysics, and I knew this was where Jacob got his books because I'd asked Scott and then Ben.

I now worked there, four nights, nine p.m. until past eleven, and then Saturdays, with room to maneuver if I needed to be present for a game. I shared duties with a chemistry guy called Johan Spokes who played baseball, so we worked out our schedules between us.

This was Mom's idea, one of many.

Top of the list, she'd advised, was to get a job, be useful, see how much time it stole from studying and playing. Dad hadn't been overly impressed at first. His reasoning was that I didn't need to work on anything but my skating if I really wanted to play top-tier hockey. I think maybe Ten slapped him or something because there was this noise, then some muttering, and then Dad saying that he actually fully endorsed me experiencing the world.

Of course, he didn't know the bit about Jacob and the real reason why I wanted to work.

Not that I was even sure why this was a good idea, but Mom had suggested that if I worked nine-to-five, then I could be a friend who cared. Or something. She got that I didn't want to look shallow, but didn't have an answer when I'd asked her if me taking this job was depriving another student of the ability to earn money?

God, my head was so screwed.

I'd been there for two weeks, and he hadn't been in, and I'd even gone through his book list and pulled out what I could find before hiding them at the back of the shelves so no one else took them. No one knew what I was doing, not even Scott and Ben, who took my excuse of needing studying time as true.

"I'm done," Johan said and wiped his hands on his jeans. We'd been going through boxes of donations, and how books could get that dirty was beyond even me. "Later."

I sketched a wave and crouched down to get the next loads of donations sorted, snorting a laugh when I found a very '70s version of *The Joy of Sex* and three *Playgirl* magazines. I wasn't sure self-help books or porn, were what the shop was looking for from leaving students, but never mind.

"What are you doing?"

I stood immediately at hearing Jacob's soft growl behind me. "Working," I defended quickly and tried to slow the rapid beating of my heart. *He just surprised me, is all.*

He stared at the books in my hand, then up at me, and I dropped them into the box, feeling my face heat up.

"Working," he repeated.

I was at a loss at what else to say and instead tugged his sleeve and pulled him over to the bookshelf at the back of the store. "Look," I demanded and let go of him to pull out the botany books that hid all of the ones I'd found on his list.

He peered at them and then pulled out the first one. "*Crop Rotation on Organic Farms*," he read out the title and looked bemused.

"Yeah, I didn't know. Maybe you've already covered that, but I did some research." I pulled out another equally thick tome, "*Organic Principles and Practices* isn't on your list, but it's supposed to give you an alternate view." I cleared my throat after that because he was staring at me as if I was a puzzle he needed to solve.

"Why did you do this?"

Was he pissed? I couldn't tell.

"It's what friends do," I said and drew my shoulders back in readiness for a fight.

His expression changed. He was tense, angry maybe? He turned away from me.

"I don't need a friend," he bit out and stalked to the door, opening it and then slamming it so hard I thought the glass would fall out.

Disappointment sliced through me, but I was a Madsen, and I wasn't going to give up. Still, it burned, and my eyes were wet, and I felt like a fucking idiot.

The door slammed open again, and then Jacob strode toward me. The nearer he got, the tenser I felt, and then he was on me, near hip-checking me into the stack, and then he kissed me. Consumed me. Held me so tight I couldn't breathe. I scrambled for purchase, finally gripping his shirt and pawing at him in the passion of the moment. He gentled the kiss a little and then moved back, but I wouldn't let him go.

"I don't want a friend," he said.

I tightened my grip on his shirt. I didn't want to hear him say that was our last kiss.

"Jacob, please—"

He kissed me again. Like a starving man, he took and he took and he held me close.

"I'm sorry," he repeated over and over again into the kisses. Then finally he backed away. "I'm sorry I got so angry on the ice, but I want the Ryker Madsen from the summer, and I can't have you, and I hate that. I want to be more than friends, God help me, I want to be good enough. I don't know why you want me, but I need way more."

I reached up and cradled his cheek, and he pushed into my touch.

"We should get out of here," I said.

"When do you finish work?" he asked and turned his head to kiss my hand.

I was weak at the knees, and I wanted his lips back on mine. I know he'd asked me a question, but I wasn't listening. The door opened, and a group of students walked in, talking loudly and rummaging through boxes by the door. I'd forgotten I was even at work. Thank goodness he reminded me because I was new at this working business.

"I'm done at eleven," I said.

"I'll be outside."

He pressed one last kiss to my hand and left without a backward glance, and now I had to decide how I was going to serve people with a hard-on.

Thank God for long hockey jerseys.

TWELVE

Jacob

TIMES LIKE THIS I WISHED I HAD A BARN TO MUCK OUT. BY hand. But there were no barns on campus, so I paced outside the bookstore while chewing gum. By the time Ryker was locking up to join me, I'd chewed a whole pack of spearmint gum. The aroma of spearmint would probably be leeching out of my pores for days. We stood there under a skinny fall moon, staring at each other, smiling like dolts.

"Want to walk to your place?"

I shook my head. "There's zero privacy at the house. Can we go to your dorm?"

He took me by the hand and led me to Tamarack Hall, the newest dormitory on campus. We rode in the elevator to the top floor, fingers intertwined, sneaking glances at each other. Nerves made me feel slightly sick. The hallway we exited into was bright and clean, the smell of fresh paint and new carpeting lingering in the air.

Ryker had the end apartment, a posh suite with a huge lounge area and a corner window setup that looked down onto the whole campus. I dropped his hand. He moved around to turn on a light on the end table. I padded to the window, stunned by the rich elegance surrounding me. Then he was beside me, pulling on my arm, leading my attention back to him. I swept him into me, crushing him to my chest, and began kissing him like a man possessed. We fumbled to the bedroom, touching and tasting as we went.

I wasn't quite sure how I'd been so lucky to get this second chance, but I was not about to fuck it up. Or I hoped I didn't fuck it up, but knowing me, I probably would with my big, rough, grasping hands or my lack of poetic praise for his beauty.

"Jacob, are you still into this?" Ryker's voice was hot and breathy beside my ear, his hands roaming over my back under my shirt.

I pulled away from his neck and the warm patch of skin under his ear that I'd been savoring. "I feel I'm not worthy of your forgiveness." He rolled his eyes so hard it was a wonder he didn't sprain them. That made me smile, and a bit of the worry and uneasiness melted away. "Okay, yeah, stupid, I know."

"Totally stupid." He walked me to the bed, his big one, the extra-firm double with the fancy Egyptian cotton sheets of cool blue that probably cost more than our haybine and—shit, I had to stop that bullshit. I had to stop feeling like a lesser man because of where I came from and what I was. I was just as good as Ryker Madsen. I was just as good as anyone on this campus. I was. Wasn't I?

"Tell me I'm good enough," I whispered, skidding to a halt with the bed just a few inches away. He blinked. I grimaced and shook my head. "Forget that came out of me."

"No, hell no, I'm not forgetting that. How could I?"

I released his lean hips so that I could shove my fingers into his hair… oh man… that hair of his. Luxurious and thick, soft on the work-hewn callouses on my fingertips, his beautiful hair that smelled of wishes fulfilled and hot summer nights.

"Like this." I covered his mouth with mine before he could protest. He was stiff and still now, obviously not ready to give up the conversation that I'd blundered into during a moment of utter weakness. He pulled free of the kiss, but I chased his puffy lips, mad to get lost in him... to show him that I was worthy of his affection, his admiration, his love.

"Jacob, we need to talk—"

"No, no talking. Not about that. Not about anything but what you want in bed, okay? Please, Ryker, please let me show you how much... I just. Fuck. I want to be with you tonight. We can talk in the morning, okay?" I held his head in my hands as I spoke, my gaze locked with his. I could see the turmoil in his thoughts as they played out over his face. Then the tension left his brow, and his eyes softened. He nodded gently, lifting his mouth for another kiss, which I gave him with a passion that burned so brightly there would have been no way to form words even if I'd wanted to, which I didn't.

We hit the bed in a wild knot of legs and arms, his lips leaving mine only for as long as it took to pull his shirt over his head or for him to find and tug down my jogging pants. Grunting and cursing when his zipper got stuck on the cotton of his underwear, he laughed at my snarling comment about cutting him out of his fucking jeans with my jackknife. That heated chuckle of his and the battle with the zipper lowered the madness just a bit. With a jerk that busted the zipper, I finally got him freed of the denim and his underwear. I threw the clothing over my shoulder and sat back on my calves, between his legs, and stared down at the man now lying under me, naked and pink with desire.

"I love how you're made," I said, my voice shaky and odd to my ears. His cock was hard as granite, weeping slightly. I ran my hands up his chest to his wide shoulders and then down his sides, my fingertips bumping over his ribs, then coming to rest on his hips. "I love how you're made."

"You said that already." He reached over his head, his hands sliding under the pillows as he stretched for me, elongating his firm, lean body even more.

"I think I'm dumbstruck." I bent over to tongue his navel.

He gasped and snorted, his hips rising from the bed.

"Oh man, that tickles," he sniggered and writhed, not really pulling away despite his claim that he was ticklish. "You were always dumb."

"Mm, I know. I nearly lost you. That's about as dumb as a man can be." I speared his bellybutton again and then licked my way down to his cock. Knowing I should stretch this out more but not having a fucking clue how to extend the foreplay, I did my best not to fall on his cock like a starving man. I licked and teased, lapped at his prick from the fat head to the base, fondling his nuts as he grunted and mewled, his hips flicking upward whenever my lips neared his cockhead. I rubbed my face along his cock, releasing his balls to apply a bit of pressure to his taint. His heels dug into the mattress as a low, deep sound of pleasure rumbled out of him.

"Oh fuck, that's—do that again."

So I did. I rubbed on that area, making wider and wider circles as I nibbled on his prick like it were a cob of Silver Queen corn fresh from my mother's garden. God knows he was as salty and sweet as that summer treat. When my index finger brushed his hole, his whole body convulsed.

"More, more, more," Ryker panted, pulling on the sheets, popping the fitted one under us away from the corner. His legs were bent, deeply, as he gyrated manically in an attempt to give me more room between his thighs. I settled in there, licking at the juncture of his leg and his body, inhaling the musky smell of Ryker mixed with the lingering scent of his soap. All the while I toyed with his ass, pressing on his opening as I tasted and teased his dick, my own cock weeping and leaving wet spots on the expensive sheets. "Give me more. I want you inside me. Get inside me. I want you inside me."

I lifted my head from his inner thigh and looked right at him. He was flushed and sweaty, his eyes glazed with lust and his lips swollen from my kisses.

"Are you sure?" I asked, my throat suddenly tight.

"Yeah, totally sure."

He *looked* sure. I was now utterly terrified. "I've never done that with anyone…"

Ryker smiled. It was as if the sun had burst to life in the middle of the night. "I've been with a couple of girls. It's got to be the same. Dick goes into hole, right?"

"Okay, right, I guess so."

It was not at *all* the same.

Ryker seemed to be slightly mistaken in a few key aspects of hot gay butt sex as it compared to hot bi vagina sex. First thing that we stumbled across was that Ryker was so tense that even getting a slick finger into him was difficult.

"Ouch. No, stop. That's not right. More lube," he grunted several times. I grabbed the pump bottle and covered his ass. He was now lying in a puddle of Astroglide the size of a small dorm fridge. His ass, balls, cock, and thighs were shiny with lubricant. Lube coated my arm from my hand to my elbow.

"I've seen fisting videos with less lube," I mumbled as I eyed my right hand. Ryker snorted in amusement, then inhaled sharply as I pressed my index finger into him. He jerked and rolled his head side to side, his legs slowly falling open. I took that as a cue that we'd finally done something that pleased him. So I lay back down, took the head of his cock into my mouth, grimaced at the taste of lube, and worked my finger in and out of his ass.

"Yeah, yeah, good, oh shit yeah good. No, fuck, shit!" He blew apart in my mouth with a fury that made me hotter than hell. I swallowed quickly, pushing my finger into his ass deeper and then hooking it a bit to find his sweet spot. When I bumped the knot of nerves, he cried out in bliss, filling my mouth with another spurt. I worked his prostate and cock like that for several minutes, milking him out, taking every droplet of cum and savoring it. When he began breathlessly begging for me to stop, I pulled my finger out of his ass and popped off his soft cock. I crawled over him and kissed him, sweeping deeply into his mouth.

He kissed me back languidly, spent and satisfied, his nose wrinkling when the taste of him coated his own tongue.

"I taste gross," he huffed as I rocked my cock into his thigh, trying to find enough friction to get myself off.

"You taste incredible," I murmured while licking my way to his neck, pumping my ass furiously. He took me in hand and finished me off with five hard jerks. I blew my load all over his thigh. When the tremors subsided, I fell off him, my cock leaving a wet trail over his hip bone.

"We have a phenomenal mess." Ryker wiggled out of reach and left the bed. I was too boneless to move so I lay there, face in the mattress, floating on the afterglow of amazing sex with the man I couldn't live without. "Come on, man, get up so we can change the sheets."

He slapped my ass when I refused to move. I sprang up then, grabbing him around the waist. We pushed and pulled, laughing softly, until we were in the shower . Man, this was a nice place. Big and roomy with zero roommates barging in, making messes, bringing home women and then making them squeal all night long. In his dorm, it was just him and me. We fell into the shower, still grappling like Greco-Roman wrestlers as the water beat down on us. I simply overpowered him in the end, but not by much. His back to the tiled wall, I kissed him into submission, his fingers knotting up in my wet hair.

"I missed you." He sighed when the kissing slowed.

"I missed you too." I washed him off, working the soap into a thick lather, then caressing every inch of him with soapy palms. He snickered as I used the tips of my fingers on his cheeks and around his eyes, sighed when I washed his back, and groaned when I lathered up his heavy sac. "Don't ever let me be that stupid again."

"Right, like I can stop the stupid from coming out of you."

He soaped me and rinsed me and even dried me. I took the towel from him and threw it into the hamper, and then pulled him back into the bedroom. We stripped the bedding, put on clean sheets, and then settled under the fresh linen, his leg resting on mine as if it were crafted to be there. His hair was still wet. Tiny rivulets of water ran over my biceps onto the pillowcase. It was good. It was all good. Who cared if the pillowcase was damp? Not me. The whole bed could've been submerged in water, and I'd have been unaware of the wetness. Ryker and I were in bed again. He was curled into my side, chattering about school or hockey or... who knew.

"Are you?"

I ran my finger around his ear, lost in the pleasure of his warm skin resting next to mine.

"Sorry, what?"

"You're so typical. Blow a nut and fall asleep."

"Yeah, well, you're a guy. You should be ready for sleep too."

"I'm a civilized man. I talk and cuddle after sex. So, are you staying here or going home?" He ran a hand over my stomach, his fingers coming to rest on my sternum.

"You okay with me staying?" My heart was beating a little faster than normal. This was something I'd kind of dreamed off, waking up with Ryker, sexing him up, then feeding him something that I'd made with all-natural, farm-raised ingredients. The two of us sitting on the front porch, his hand in mine, as the sun rose pink and purple over Minnesota.

"Yeah, I'd like that." He yawned so widely his jaw cracked.

"Looks like your civilized cuddle man wants to crash just like my caveman does." He burrowed into my side, mumbling to himself, which made me smile at the now dark room. "I'll be here when you wake up."

"Cool." He went lax then, his breathing evening out and his head growing heavier. With him sound asleep on my arm, I stared at the ceiling for a moment, closed my eyes, and drifted off into that dream of me, Ryker, and a summer morning on the farm.

THIRTEEN

Ryker
_____

OUR FIRST GAME AGAINST LEICESTER CAME AROUND WAY TOO
quickly. Five below us in our division, they weren't exactly
fighting for points, but I knew it was going to be a hard game.
I'd already had a couple of texts from the few people I kept in
contact with, and they didn't make good reading.

How was I supposed to take a text from Paulie, winger,
asshole, super religious anti-gay, that simply said, *we're
waiting for you, Mads*? He added a smile and a winky face, as
if that made it any less of a threat, but then he'd lived his
whole life that way.

Hey homo. Smile, smile, winky face.

Is Ten the girl, or is it your dad? Smile, smile, winky face.

At first, I gave the emojis some weight, thought maybe he
didn't mean his shit, but no. He really did mean the crap he
came out with. God help him if he got up in Benoit's face
with all his crap about slavery and social rights. He was the
kind of asshole who would ask straight-faced questions about
Ben's ancestors.

I sent back a standard, *we're on our way*, but left off any
bright yellow faces.

"What can you tell us?" John Crowley, Owatonna captain and an all-round nice guy, leaned over his seat and stared right at me.

I needed to sum up a team I'd never felt right on and pick up any little gaps the Eagles could take advantage of. In my bones, I was convinced that we could win tonight just from my work I was so focused on showing them what a real team could look like. I could imagine scoring on them, out-dangling them, making them appear like amateurs.

"They're easily confused," I summarized. "The Lions don't talk to each other, no communication at all except constant shouting, and they take offense at anything you do to them really quick."

"Okay. And the goalie, this Richards guy?"

The bus winding its way to Leicester turned off the freeway and lurched enough for John to cling to the seat.

"Jeez, Scott, your dad is pushing it a bit," John called over to Scott, who slid down in his seat with a cap pulled over his eyes. The team ragged on Scott a lot for his dad's eagerness to get to games. The drives back were always slower unless we lost. Then they were slower but ragged. He didn't need to drive the bus for money. It was all voluntary, and the bus itself had been a donation from him to the team. He was fully invested in Scott's hockey future, which from what I had seen was all kinds of shiny.

"So yeah, Richards?" John prompted.

"Solid, but go high. Statistically, he's low in the net for the first period, and if you can get three goals done, then you'll start to rattle him."

"Anything else?"

"Their chirping is loud. They pick up on any of your shit, so you need to stay calm."

John narrowed his eyes and leaned over. "They give you

crap?" He looked briefly at Jacob who was next to Scott and staring out of the window. Jacob and I hadn't made a grand announcement to the team about being a couple, but one touch at the wrong time, and John had put two and two together. He'd pulled us both to one side, told us not to let it fuck up the hockey or indeed our college stuff, and then hugged us both. It seemed like the whole team knew now, but no one appeared to have a problem with it. Well, if they did, it wasn't to our faces, and they didn't show it in any of the practices this last week. Tonight was the litmus test, I guessed. See if the team cohesion I loved about the Owatonna Eagles would hold up against the Leicester Lions.

John sat back down, which was good because we were only ten minutes from the campus, and I needed that to get my game face on. I glanced over at Jacob, who had his nose in a book until maybe he sensed I was watching, and looked at me. He quirked a smile and then winked before heading back to the book.

I wished we could've sat together, but seats on the team bus had already been dealt with by the time I'd arrived. Tradition, luck, they all played a part in who a team member sat next to. Jacob and Scott were next to each other, Ben a little farther forward with Sam Gagnon, the other goalie, and I was stuck next to Dawson Richardson, whose only fault was that he wasn't Jacob.

The bus pulled into the campus, reversed into a space, and the engine turned off.

We all bundled off, grabbing bags and all the things that made the long bus journeys great, like snacks, iPads with movies or handheld games, and finally, when there was nothing more for me to collect, I was the last person off the bus. Leicester smelled different from Owatonna—that was the first thing I thought. The next feeling I had was shock as someone jumped me, squealing in my ear then pushing me back against the bus and kissing me. My hands instinctively moved to push, and finally, I managed to get the kisser off me.

She stood back, hands on her lips, scarlet lipstick smudged.

"You asshole!" She slapped my chest, and I winced. Not in pain, but at the fact that not more than ten seconds off the bus and Natalie had found me. Natalie whom I'd dated for two months at the end of my final semester at Leicester. Natalie who never stopped talking about how gorgeous Ten was and when could she meet him because all he needed was to meet her and he wouldn't be gay anymore. "You never call or text, and what was with blocking me on Twitter."

I gaped at her. I hadn't actually been on Twitter since I'd gone to Owatonna, so that answered that one. And why would I call her?

"Last time we spoke, I told you that no, I wouldn't introduce you to Ten and that we were done."

Her expression changed then, from playful pushing to soulful heartbroken diva-ness.

"Awww, Ryk-eeee, don't say things like that. I forgive you. We can go back to dating."

Oh god, not this again. I glanced past her at Jacob, whose expression was unreadable. We'd never talked about my time at Leicester. Well, we had, but only in a hockey sense, not in the way of explaining an ex-whatever-she-was.

"We were never dating," I said, loud enough for Jacob to hear. Of course, that meant the whole freaking team heard, and there were some sniggers. Great. Jacob though? He just looked at me, and then he did that eyebrow-raising thing which I found so cute.

Jacob. I'm with Jacob.

She moved closer. "I call what we had definitely dating," she said, and very carefully I eased her away.

"No, it wasn't. I have hockey to play."

She didn't move, so how the hell did I get her to back away? This was ridiculous, and now I could see Coach Quinton join the huddle around us. This was going from bad to fucking worse.

"But we had something," she said.

"No, we didn't. You wanted to make Ten straight, remember? You just wanted me to get you in his bed, or did you forget that?"

Her eyes narrowed, and I knew I'd maybe said the wrong thing. She wasn't back at being vicious.

She pouted and tossed her long, blonde hair, then turned dramatically to my team. "He doesn't want this. Then he's gay. Don't you think so, boys?" She cocked her hip a little, and I bet she was throwing one of those looks where she thought she was gorgeous. Duck face, I think it was called.

Silence. I died inside.

"No," Scott said, and his tone was thoughtful, but his expression focused. "I think he's technically bi. Don't you think so, Ben?"

Ben nodded, crossing his arms over his chest, "Yep, bi is what he is, not gay. I think he's pretty certain about that."

She huffed then, caught out on what the hell to say next, and then she rounded on me.

"Whatever," she snapped and then left.

No one hurried to say anything. Scott slapped my shoulder, Ben hip checked me so hard I stumbled away, and Jacob smiled at me.

All was well in my world.

· · ·

THE GAME WASN'T PARTICULARLY HARD. It was messy and uncoordinated on the Lions' side, their defense was all over the place, and we were two to their zero at the end of the first period. One of those goals was mine. The other was a beautiful top shelf from John, off a pass from Scott. Our line was on fire, and Ben in goal saved any shots that came his way with ease. I could see the tension in the Lions, remembered what it was like to be there last year. The coach would be yelling, demanding more, but never giving guidance on how to get more. The cohesion was lacking, and with only ten minutes to go to the end of the game, they'd only managed to get one goal back, a blatant shove on Ben that a ref somehow missed. Maybe he felt sorry for them, who knew. There were a couple of near misses from our forwards; three that ended up hitting the pipes. One from Scott that I couldn't believe hadn't found its way past the Lions' goalie.

Two minutes to go, and we were on a power play after one of their defensemen was called for tripping. The ice was dirty, the puck wild, and my line was out, John passing to Scott, and to me, and the check that pushed me into the boards was enough to steal my breath but not enough to take the puck. One thing I'd been working on with Jacob was getting trapped in the corner and working the puck free, and all I had to do was imagine how I was stuck and focus on getting out of there.

I didn't even hear the chirps the Lion's D-man was giving me. It was all noise, and with the strength I had in my legs, I pushed back and away, corralling the dancing puck and shoving it out to Jacob, whom I knew would be there, waiting. I could feel it, knew it was right, and he collected the puck, passed it to John, who cannoned it to Scott, and with ten seconds left on the clock, Scott went five-hole on the goalie, and we'd scored again.

When the buzzer sounded, we'd won six-one, and I didn't even hear the booing in the arena. I was on a high which lasted all the way to the bus where Scott's dad, Gordy, waited. I saw Scott bound over to him, smiled because I knew how proud Dad would be of me if I'd played as well as Scott had tonight. Two goals and so many chances, he'd been a demon on the ice.

But Gordy didn't look happy. In fact, he looked pissed, and I saw in the slump of Scott's shoulders how he was taking that as his dad talked at him.

"What's the story with Scott and his dad?" I asked Ben, who sighed.

"His dad will be pissed he only got two goals." He shook his head. "I don't know who's harder on Scott; his dad or Scott himself. High expectations, you know."

On the way home I texted a summary of the game to Dad, talked about Scott, and how my corner work had improved after working with Jacob. He would get them later, as I knew the Railers were playing Boston tonight. A big game for the Rowe brothers, with Ten's brother being the captain of the Boston team. He would reply later, but it wouldn't be admonishing me for not scoring; it would be praise for my work, maybe even suggestions on how to beat a determined defenseman. Of course, if I were talking to my grandfather, he would have comments about me not scoring, but then he was one generation removed, and he wanted me to be some hockey phenom as Ten was.

I glanced at Scott who'd taken the window seat and was staring out. He looked defeated, and that was sad. Jacob caught my gaze and half smiled, and I mouthed "Is Scott okay?" He nodded but also frowned, so that told me a lot.

By the time we were back at Owatonna, Scott was back to his usual self, closing Jacob's textbook and harassing him about cows. Or that is what it sounded like from my seat. At least Jacob was smiling.

I loved his smile.

BEN WOULDN'T LET it alone.

"Come to the party, J," he said for what must have been the tenth time since Scott decided it was pool party time at his house. God knows what that would be like in the Minnesota winter, but I guessed it was heated and maybe undercover. "You know it's important to him."

"He shouldn't be doing this."

I guess Jacob meant drinking when school was hard work and hockey even harder, but I think I was missing something.

Scott lived only ten miles or so from the campus, in a place that sounded bigger than Stan's massive home. I don't know what his dad did, but the house and the fact he was always around Owatonna U with the driving and support for the team was an indication that maybe he didn't have to work.

Maybe it was old money. Who knew?

Scott announced that morning that his parents were away for a family wedding and that tonight, a typically ordinary Friday evening, with no game or practice, it was party time at his place.

The whole idea sounded cool, but Jacob was studying for his gen chem class, and the only time he stopped studying was when we were in bed or playing hockey. I never pushed it, but today I'd noticed the way he kept frowning and then pressing his fingers to his temples. He needed a night to play, to work off some of the stress, and I was determined tonight was that night. I was playing the slow game, using all my wiles to get him to go, but Ben was right up in his face about it.

So I got in the middle of the two of them and placed a hand on Jacob's firm chest. "I totally understand you need to study, but maybe, if you drive, we go for a couple of hours, and you can go for a swim. With me." I added the last as an incentive and saw him soften at the words. Alone time was sparse for us both, maybe we just needed some fun.

"Half an hour," he said, more to the hovering Ben than to me.

"Two hours," Ben countered.

"One," I compromised, and saw the moment Jacob caved because he smiled that gorgeous smile of his, and that was it. I knew I would be able to get him to chill for a bit.

We arrived at Scott's place a while after the party had started, and beer was flowing, and the core of the team was in the kitchen devouring delivered pizzas. A gallery of photos covered the wall of the corridor from the kitchen—all three children taken from when they were babies up to the present day. I recognized Scott in all of them, and it seemed he had a younger sister and an older brother. Towards the end, there were lone shots of the brother, and I saw enough of him with various cups that it prompted me to ask Scott a question.

"Does your brother play professionally?"

"He died when he was seventeen," Scott said, very simple and to the point. "Let's go." He pushed past me to the back door and opened it to the frigid air outside. I took the hint that he didn't want to discuss it, and I knew enough not to push. Jacob went out first, and he was a lot harder than I was because, shit, it was cold enough to freeze fire.

"And the pool is heated, right?" I was dubious because

firstly, I couldn't see steam rising from it, and secondly, it was entirely open to the elements, not in a building at all.

Scott took all his clothes off except his boxers and grinned at me. "No!" he shouted, and with a whoop, he ran for the pool and divebombed into it. Water splashed us, icy water, and I stepped back. No way was I jumping in there, so my image of Jacob and me smooching in warm water on a cold night with the stars above us was thrown out the window.

"Is he gonna freeze to death?" I asked, and yeah, I was more than worried. Scott wasn't moving, he was floating on his back, and that shit had to be really bad for him.

Jacob crouched at the edge. "Come on, man, get out."

"It—it—it's hot," Scott's teeth were chattering, which made a lie of his words.

"Scott, come on, man…"

I'd seen Scott down three beers in the half hour we'd been there. Was this a bad thing? I took my phone out of my pocket and put it on the patio table, prepared to jump in and force Scott out.

"No—no—" Scott said, and his voice was soft and so full of pain.

Jacob reached out a hand. "Come out, or I'm coming in, and you know I can't swim well."

Scott didn't move for a short while. Then in a flurry of motion, he made it to the side and allowed Jacob to pull him out. Jacob marched him into the house, and I picked up my phone and followed him in.

What the hell had that been about? Was the dude that drunk, or was he just fucking insane?

The party didn't go on for long after that. Most of the guys were wary, and Scott had vanished to his room, wrapped in a large towel Jacob had gotten him. In fact, Jacob had gone with him, which left me and the rest of the team waiting on what came next.

"What was that about?" I asked in general. There was some muttering, but Ben was the one who took point.

"His brother drowned," Ben answered. "He was on spring break, got pulled out by a riptide. They found his body three days later. Scott was only fourteen or so then."

Shit. That was terrible. All of a sudden, I wanted to go home and hug my sisters, all three of the cute monsters who had my heart in their hands. I was shaky and unsure of myself... hell, of life in general at that moment. I'd heard my grandfather say that life was short and all that "old people" talk, but I'd never imagined losing someone in my family. I wasn't sure I could imagine it, to be honest. I guess I *was* the protected rich boy Jacob had said I was.

When Jacob came out, he ushered the team out until it was just him and me there.

"You can go with them," he said. "I want to stay here for Scott."

"Is he okay?"

"He will be, but if he needs someone, I want to be here."

"I'll stay as well."

I sat on the nearest sofa and pulled out my phone, resolving to FaceTime my Mom and sisters, or Ten and Dad. Jacob clearly had something he wanted to say, and then he just sighed and took the facing sofa where he had stowed his backpack and took out one of his ever-present books.

We were there for Scott, and we were together. Seeing my sisters sleeping, which was all Mom could show me given it was midnight, was enough to make me smile. Due to the time, I also didn't bother contacting Dad and Ten, just checked out some photos of all of us I had on the phone.

And like that, with Jacob studying quietly, I fell asleep at Scott's house.

FOURTEEN

Jacob

I'D GOTTEN A NIGHT OFF FROM WORK. I'D KIND OF WANTED A nap and a couple of hours to work on an assignment for my Agricultural Law class, but Ryker Madsen. Yeah, he'd found me in the library, hidden in a corner, and coerced me into putting aside my books for an hour. One hour. That was what he'd vowed. Then he'd sealed that vow with a sweet kiss that made me hard as a fire poker.

"One hour on the ice to work on getting the puck out of the corners. I've got an hour saved for us. I even bribed Fizzy, the Zamboni guy, so that he'd have fresh ice for us."

"Ryker..." I sighed, my lips still tingling from our kiss. "I don't have an hour to spare."

He pouted, pretty eyes all sad, and I knew I was done.

"Okay, one hour."

His frown turned into a brilliant smile. We gathered up my books and laptop and walked briskly across the campus to the rink. Our breath clouded in front of us as we hustled along, Ryker talking nonstop about this and that, hockey, classes, Ten and his father, the latest trending show on

Netflix. I burrowed farther into my coat, the icy wind burning my cheeks as it blew across the quad.

Ice time was precious, and I thought to ask what he'd bribed Fizzy with because Fizzy was notorious for being a son of a bitch. He was kind of the Argus Filch of Owatonna University. Always ratting out students and athletes to faculty and coaching staff. Ryker had probably waved a Tennant Rowe-signed jersey or something under Fizzy's hawk like nose. I thought to ask, but by then we were changing into our gear, Ryker babbling on steadily until we were on the ice.

"Okay," he said, his mouthguard in his gloved hand, his helmet on his head. The flow was incredible. I reached out to touch all that silky hair escaping his helmet. Ryker's eyes glowed with passion and not for hockey. "Dude, none of that right now. Later. After dinner."

"Dinner?"

"Oh, what? Yeah, Ten and Dad are flying in for the game against the Wild. They'll be here at seven, and we're doing dinner."

"When was all this decided?"

"About two hours ago. You'll love them. Don't freak out. Okay, so I need you to lean on me hard, okay? I'm sloppy in the corners, weak. I need to learn how to handle big guys like you."

"Ryker, I think you already know how to handle big guys like me. Remember that hand job last night?" I reached for his hair again.

He swatted my hand away, but desire still burned in his gaze. "Dude, focus. Hockey. We're here for hockey. Now, try to take the puck from me."

He skated off, puck on his stick, and I sighed and followed it into the corner. I hit him hard, not as hard as I could have, but hard enough that the glass shook. Then I took the puck from him and slapped it down the ice.

"Fucker. Fucking shitty fucker!" He pounded on the glass, skated off to fetch the puck, and we did it again. And again. And again.

"You're trying to be too fancy," I told him after overpowering him in the corner for the tenth time. "Stop trying to outmaneuver me. You can't once I get my weight into you. Use your size to lever me off-balance, then go for the fancy."

He nodded, and we went at it again, in the corner, sweaty and snarling, pushing hard against each other, battling for possession of a little chunk of black rubber. Ryker met me shove for shove, elbow for elbow, hip to hip, using his strength and size to keep his face from the glass. Then, with a slick move that Tennant would've been proud of, he squirted away from me, spinning and kicking the puck free, leaving me in his dust because there was no way I could catch him. He slapped the puck into the visitors net, crowed and shouted, pumping the air. I plowed into him, driving him into the boards, and covered his mouth with mine.

He kissed me back with fire. Sticks fell to the ice, as did gloves. I ripped at his helmet, drove my fingers into his wet hair, and pressed my groin into his.

"I don't recall ever seeing *that* on any of your defensive zone coverage schematics on that whiteboard," someone said loudly with some thick humor.

Ryker shoved me away. I turned to look at Tennant and Jared standing on the ice about three feet from us. Heat raced up my neck to my face.

"I'm not sure how well accepted that kind of defending would be in the NHL," Jared replied to his boyfriend, a wry sort of smile on his face.

"We were working in the corners," Ryker said, shuffling out from behind me.

"Yeah, I saw that. Corner work now has a whole new meaning." Tennant chuckled, pulling Ryker out to hug him soundly. I shifted my weight from one skate to the other as they embraced.

"You guys weren't supposed to be here until seven," Ryker said, gliding back to stand beside me. "This is Jacob. We're kind of... dating."

"I assumed as much," Jared said dryly. "Otherwise I'd be pulling you aside to ask what kind of defensive drills this school is teaching you."

Ryker snickered. Tennant held out his hand. We shook. Then Jared and I also shook.

"I'm weak in the corners, and Jacob was helping me," Ryker explained.

Tennant gave Ryker a long look. "You want me to skate up and give you some pointers?"

My mouth may have fallen open just a bit. "We'd love that," I blurted out. "I mean tips from a pro are always good."

"Then let's play a bit, and then we'll hit the Chinese. I'm in dire need of some lobster and coconut fried rice," Tennant called as he shuffled over the ice in his sneakers.

"Does he have skates with him wherever he goes?" I whispered into Ryker's ear.

"Usually, yeah. The man was born with a hockey stick in his hand."

"Wow."

Jared gave me a long look, not a mean, assessing one, but a highly curious, calculating appraisal. Ryker chatted on about this and that until Ten returned and handed Jared some old skates.

"Put them on," Ten shoved the skates at his boyfriend.

"Let's see if you two rough and tough D-men can keep us slick forwards pinned in the corner."

"Tennant, I'm really not sure I feel like…" Jared began.

"Oh, hey, what now? Are you like too tired to skate a little. Damn, I'm sorry, Gramps. Shall we call the nurse for some prune juice and to turn on *Murder, She Wrote* before you go to bed at seven o'clock?"

Jared threw Tennant a sour glare. Then the corners of his mouth twitched. "Fine. But don't whine when you're on your ass."

Yeah, that Tennant being on his ass boast? Never. Happened. I mean, not once. Jared and I had all we could do to keep Rowe in the corner, let alone being able to maul on him or knock him to his ass. The man was incredibly nimble, quick as lightning, and able to make defenders and even his fellow forwards look like fools. Ryker tried, I mean he really tried, but he was no way close to the skater that Tennant Rowe was.

"Is it time for Chinese yet?" Ten shouted after stealing the puck from Jared and me, then socking it into the net, again, for like the fortieth time.

"Yeah, I'm fine with calling it a day," Jared panted, pulling in hot, hard breaths just the same as I was.

"Cool! We'll meet you outside in like twenty so you can scrub because you two reek," Tennant skated off, stick over his shoulder, hardly sweaty or winded at all, as if the past thirty minutes had been leisure time for him.

"It'll take me that long to catch my breath," Jared joked, following his man.

"Do you think Tennant is like some sort of alien or something?" I asked Ryker as we hurried to dress after a fast shower where we did not touch each other, but we sure looked longingly at each other. "I mean, is he from some planet where they all were ice gods, and he was sent to earth by his parents when his planet was going to blow up."

"That's totally *Superman* aside from the ice god bit."

"Yeah, I know. My point stands."

"You're an ass." Ryker shimmied up close to steal a kiss. "It's nice to see you loosening up a little."

"Don't get used to it. Playing around in the corners doesn't get my assignments done or—"

He rose to his toes to press his lips to mine again, effectively silencing me.

"Leave school shit for tonight, okay? Just give me a couple more hours of this laid-back Jacob before serious Jacob returns."

I slid an arm around his waist, tugging him tight to me. "Am I really that bad?"

"You're totally that bad, but it's one of the things that I… like about you."

"I like that you're totally not serious."

"Hey!"

I covered his mouth with mine. He responded with fire. Pushing him against a locker and going to my knees to suck him down my throat had real merit. But there was Chinese food to be eaten and family to try to win over. Family. I wondered how mine would react to Ryker. That dream of watching a Minnesota sunrise warm his beautiful face never strayed too far away.

IT TOOK three weeks for the daydream/nightmare of seeing the glow of a Minnesota dawn on Ryker's face to become a reality. He and I had become something of a couple during those twenty-one days, growing so tight that the team made comments about us being conjoined twins, which was kind of over the top, but not by much. So, the night my mother called to make sure I was coming home in two days for my father's fifty-second birthday, Ryker was with me. We'd been playing *Commando Death Match* on his PS4 when my phone rang.

I kept the call short because I'd never mentioned Ryker to them. When I was done talking to my Mom I tossed my cell to the table beside the cold nachos and reached for my controller. Ryker snapped it away from me.

"Everything okay?" he asked, boring into me with his all-too-knowing eyes. "Are we going to your place this weekend?"

I stared at the paused game on the huge plasma wall unit. "I am."

A long moment passed. I hated myself for my weakness, but I looked at him. Yep, he was pained. It radiated off him. Well shit. "I haven't told them about you."

"Then it would be a good time to do it. You've met my Dad and Ten."

"Yeah, but…"

"My Mom knows about you."

I sighed. "You outmaneuvered me."

That killer smile appeared. Then he handed me back my controller. I lost at the war game too, for the same reason.

So Friday afternoon, after Ryker's last class, he and I threw our duffel bags behind the seat of my truck and left college behind. Our farm was about an hour from Owatonna. Ryker fiddled with my CDs, finally settling on something from Toby Keith, but not really digging the tunes.

"It's too twangy," he said several times. I grunted or said nothing, my mind on the reception we'd get from my parents. Mom would be okay, overall. Dad. Well, Dad had never been what I'd call accepting of his gay son. Actually, I think he kind of assumed it was a phase and that if he ignored it, I'd forget to like guys and just be straight. These were all assumptions though because we had never talked about my homosexuality in any way. I was outed. Things were swept under the carpet.

"Is this your farm?" Ryker asked about every barn we passed. Finally, in a small fit of ugly, I snapped at him.

"I'll fucking tell you when we're there!" I shouted, taking a sharp left on a two-lane dirt road that would lead us to our farm, eventually. The joy left his eyes. I immediately felt like shit. "Sorry. I'm just... this is—my father might be..."

"It'll be okay. The worst thing he can do is ask us to leave, right?" We sat at a stop sign that was riddled with buckshot. I was white-knuckling the steering wheel, my gaze locked on the hood of my truck. I bobbed my head. "If he does, we'll just go back to campus and chill for the weekend. No matter what happens, I'll be there by your side."

He laid his hand on my thigh, and his warmth seeped into my cold soul, warming my spirit a bit.

"Right, yeah, right." I looked to the right. He was smiling at me. I wanted to cry. "If he says anything to you, anything at all, and it makes you feel bad, tell me and we'll leave."

"It'll be fine. Now can we get there? I can't wait to see the cows."

"They're cows, Ry, not magical creatures."

His exuberance helped for a while until we actually pulled up in front of my old house and walked up onto the tired front porch.

"Look, we just don't have lots of money to fix things up, so don't be shocked when you see—"

"Dude, just stop, okay. I'm not here to see the wallpaper or paint. I'm here to see where you come from and pet cows." He nudged me in the side. I nodded sheepishly, then threw the front door open, calling to my mother. She came running out of the kitchen and hit a sudden stop when she saw Ryker at my side.

"Mom, this is Ryker. My... boyfriend." I'd not used that term before. Ryker's fingers brushed mine. "Ryker, this is my mom."

She swept down on us, arms open, hugging us both to her, then releasing us so that she could cradle Ryker's face in her hands.

"Oh, Jacob, he's just adorable. Look at this face."

"I do, as often as I can."

Mom was aglow. She patted Ryker's cheeks, then tugged us into the kitchen, where supper was almost ready.

"This is going to be a... surprise for your father, Jacob," she said while tying an apron around her lean waist. "You should have let me know you were bringing your boyfriend home with you. I could have—"

"You couldn't have done much, Mom." I grabbed a carrot slice from the cutting board and looked out of the window over the sink. The milking parlor was lit up, the evening chores underway. "I'm going to take Ryker to the barn and introduce him."

Her eyebrows tangled up like fishing line. "Maybe you should just tell him that Ryker is your friend."

"No, no lying. No hiding. Either he accepts us as a couple, or we leave," I said after swallowing my carrot bite. Ryker stood in the corner by the woodstove, quietly listening. I held out my hand to him. He worked up a sickly smile. So, he was more worried than he'd let on. I'd protect him. He didn't have to worry about that. "Let's do this."

Mom kissed us both on the cheek before letting us go. The walk to the barn was stilted and tense, Ryker at my side. We stepped into the anteroom, the pulsating hum of the milking machines like a lullaby to me. Ryker blinked at the boots and overalls I waved at, but he pulled them on over his clothes, his gaze flitting all around as we dressed.

Taking him by the wrist, I led him to the parlor where the first string of cows was lined up. His eyes rounded in awe. My father and I locked gazes. It was too loud to talk, really, but I had to assume that my hand clasping Ryker's was really all that needed to be said.

We stood there, the three of us, for what seemed like forever. My pulse was rushing through my ears so loudly it nearly wiped out the sound of the milking machine.

"You going to stand there looking, or you planning on helping?" Dad shouted at me. "Cows won't come off by themselves."

It wasn't open arms and cheek kisses, but he hadn't thrown us off the farm, so I counted it as a win and got to work. Ryker stood by the gate, opening it for the exiting cows, grinning as if he'd just walked into Willy Wonka's factory instead of an ancient milking parlor. I kind of thought maybe he and I could be something serious in that moment, the thought making the inside of my breast glow like a well-tended campfire. Yeah, maybe we *could* be something solid and everlasting. Time would tell. He did seem to like cows so, yeah, maybe.

FIFTEEN

Ryker

I CAN HONESTLY SAY I'D NEVER SEEN ANYTHING LIKE IT. OR smelled anything like it. Cows, the machinery, the sounds, the scents, the efficient way Jacob and his father worked, all fascinated me. I didn't think I'd ever make it as a farmer, but I could see the appeal in the processes. Not to mention the way Jacob's muscles bunched and released with each action. He was gorgeous, sexy, messed up with sweat and muck, and I'd never wanted to kiss him more.

I also wanted to learn how to help, not used to standing on the sidelines, but one glare from Jacob's dad, and I backpedaled as if I'd not meant to go that way at all. Jacob must have seen me moving. He side-eyed me and smiled. I think he needed the reassurance that everything was okay with me, and I smiled back straight away. I could feel the glower from Jacob's dad, the burn of it too much for me to turn and face him. So instead, I watched my boyfriend's broad back and wondered how long it would be until I could kiss him.

"Call me Neil," Jacob's dad, Neil, demanded and then gestured out of the barn door and into the darkness. "Dinner."

Jacob brushed himself down and shrugged. "Dinner it is," he said. He didn't look concerned, so perhaps me meeting his dad had gone better than expected. Maybe I wasn't going to be chopped into small pieces and fed to the pigs.

Not that Jacob's family had pigs. At least he'd never mentioned they had pigs. Maybe they did, and he just never thought to tell me his dad was a serial murderer of hockey players.

"Do you have pigs?" I asked.

"No. Chickens, geese, the cows obviously, no pigs."

That was good. Neil would need to think hard about how to get rid of my body if he killed me.

The house was filled with the scents of tomato and garlic, and my stomach rumbled in protest that it had been way too long since lunch.

"I'm just going for a shower. Back in ten," Jacob said, and I almost yanked him back.

Please don't leave me alone with Neil.

But Neil was in the shower as well, so I ended up sitting at the wooden table in the center of the warm kitchen.

"It's a shame you couldn't have visited when it was colder. Beggar's Lake freezes right over. It's where Jacob learned to skate. Not that it's a huge area, but the ice is solid enough. Maybe when you come back next time? After Christmas maybe? I guess you'll be spending Christmas with your parents?"

There was so much information in that short burst of words, and I was amazed she could do all that while concentrating on adding vegetables and chicken to the tomato sauce in the pot. Jacob didn't look much like her. He was more like his dad, tall and broad, and with the same strong features.

"I'd love to come back for pond hockey," I said, deciding

to take each conversational point in turn. "We didn't have a pond, but Dad had this area he would flood with water. He was a professional hockey player, and I was in skates as soon as I could walk."

I stopped then because I wanted to hear stories about Jacob, and I shamelessly waited for them.

She went kind of misty-eyed with memory and then left the kitchen, returning with a large scrapbook which she set in front of me. She turned a few pages, and there, front and center, there was Jacob. He couldn't have been more than four or so, head to toe in purple and gold, a large moose logo on his chest, and holding a tiny hockey stick, giving the camera the thumbs-up with his free hand.

"Isn't he cute." His mom turned to the next page. This time he was a little older, and I realized this wasn't a typical family album; this was a diary of Jacob's skating. A timer sounded over by the stove, and she left me to stir and add and shake, and I carried on looking. His allegiance to the Moose team had never waned. His jerseys just got bigger, same as he did. There were some cuttings from local papers, and the letter confirming his scholarship for Owatonna. The most recent image was of him and his mom and dad all dressed up and obviously taken on a timer because Jacob was a little blurred as if he'd been running to get in front of the camera before it captured the image

"We went out for a meal to celebrate me going to college," Jacob murmured and sat next to me, leaning in to look at the book. He smelled of strawberries, and his hair was damp; I spotted water soaked into his T-shirt. He hadn't even dried off properly, which made me think he'd come back to me as quickly as he could. That felt nice. Way more than nice.

"You look good all dressed up like that," I said, then

peeked up at his mom who was watching us. "You all do. It's a lovely family photo."

Then, to break the meaningful moment, I turned back to Jacob aged three and pulled out my phone.

"I need a photo for the guys," I said, and made a big show of getting a shot, only for Jacob to wrestle it off me and hold the phone higher than I could reach. Of course, I could climb him like a tree, but his dad appeared then, and Jacob and I tried to sit calmly. Which was difficult, given my thigh was pressed against his and my cock was hard from the play fighting and laughing and the fact he smelled so damn good.

Neil dished up the food, and, after grace, Jacob and I fell on the chicken and pasta as if it was our last meal.

Neil cleared his throat. "So, you're Ryker Madsen," he said.

I nodded, swallowing the mouthful of food I had been chewing. This was some delicious cooking, certainly better than the cafeteria food at Owatonna. "I am, sir," I confirmed.

He bobbed his head. "Your dad's Jared Madsen."

"Yes, sir."

"Saw your dad a ways back, playing for the Sabres, steady defenseman."

Neil was a man of few words, it seemed, succinct in what he wanted to say because he didn't say any more for the longest time. It didn't seem to matter as Jacob's mom was apparently an expert in filling silences. I swear she could've gotten a job with the CIA. By the time we'd eaten everything, including a buttery, crumbly apple pie, she knew everything about me, including the fact my Dad had a boyfriend.

"How things have changed." She shook her head. I waited for the bad stuff; then, the lecture on the evils of whatever she considered being bad. "Do you remember Earl?" she asked her husband.

Neil inclined his head and lifted the plates from the table, taking them to the sink.

"Poor Earl," she murmured. "He was a good man. You wouldn't find a better veterinarian, but he was alone right up until the day he died. We all knew he'd had someone he lost in his past, but it was only after his funeral when his family revealed he'd had a close friend, a man friend, he'd lost in the Vietnam War. He'd never been able to tell anyone about who he really was. Isn't that right, Neil?"

"Yes." Neil turned the tap on to wash the plates, effectively cutting himself off from the conversation.

"These days you can love who you want, most of the time." I was pleased she added the extra part because not everyone had the luxury of being with the ones they loved, and the hate I'd seen at Railers games was still there. My Dad and Ten were pioneers, but just because they had each other, it didn't mean they had it easy.

The tap turned off, and Neil turned to face us, his expression sober.

"Had an offer on the farm," he announced, and the silence was dreadful.

Jacob's mom looked distraught, and I could feel the tension in Jacob.

"Wait," Jacob said and surged to his feet. "No. You said we wouldn't sell."

Neil shrugged as if it didn't matter that he wasn't messing with everything that Jacob was working for. "If you're…" He didn't finish but nodded at me and the fact I'd unerringly found Jacob's hand to hold.

"What, Dad?" Jacob snapped. "Gay?"

Neil's eyes widened, and he shook his head. "No, god, no. I meant you're with the Madsen boy, and you might want to go and see the world, play for a decent team. You don't need this place holding you back."

Jacob shook his hand free of mine. Did he want me to stand as well? Should I stand and back him up on whatever he was deciding here? When he talked about the farm, it had been with passion. How he was going to pull it back, make it better, do this thing for the cows, or that for the chickens, or something else for the waste ground out the back that could be used for something different.

"This will be my farm."

Neil crossed his arms over his chest, and I saw Jacob doing the same. These were two stubborn men in a weird kind of face-off, and I felt utterly out of place. His mom didn't intervene though, so maybe I needed to stay quiet?

"It's a pressure you might not want," Neil began.

"I want it," Jacob interjected, and then he softened a little, "Dad, everything I am is part of this farm. It's in my blood. I have so many ideas. Please don't sell."

Neil nodded then. It seemed he did a lot of his communication without using words. I watched as both men let their arms fall to their sides.

Then his dad smiled, and god, Jacob looked the same way when he laughed, as if all the weight of the world had momentarily slipped away.

"I told them no," he said. Then he turned back to the washing up, and that was it, conversation over.

I stood, then reached for Jacob's hand, and saw his eyes suspiciously bright with emotion. He gripped my hand, then released it, and went over to help his dad.

I loved family dynamics like this, where people just knew each other and loved everything about each other.

Much as I thought I was falling in love with Jacob.

. . .

WE WERE SPENDING the Christmas break apart, which started early, him back at his farm, probably studying every minute he could, and me back to my Mom's place. I had some time with her, and then, after it was over, to my Dad's. Only a couple hundred miles separated them, and I was happy to split the time. I would get to spend the day with the presents and my little sisters, watching them so excited, and then I would move on to Dad's, where I hoped to get a lot of face-to-face time with Ten and any other Railer who happened to visit.

The Railers were playing the Arizona Raptors tonight, and I wanted to know everything from the Railers about what they felt. The Raptor's track record this year had left them solidly near the bottom of the table, only two other teams were lower. Still, it was only a third of the way through the season, and things had time to change. I watched their last game, a scrappy barely-there match against LA. Their defense was aggressive, their forwards running scared. They lacked cohesion, but I needed other people to tell me that.

So I could make more of a difference when I got there.

My phone vibrated with an incoming FaceTime from Jacob, and I answered immediately, lying on my bed in my Mom's house, and desperate to hear from him. How stupid was it that I missed the sound of his voice or his steadying presence? We might not have been together, but we spent a reasonable amount of time on the phone. I knew his mom wanted me to visit again. I also knew his dad described me as "not that bad", which I took as a compliment.

"Ready?" he asked as I propped the phone up next to me.

"As I'll ever be," was my standard answer. I didn't want to watch the Raptors. This was the second matchup with them this season, and the last game had been a mess. It seemed to me that their big D-Man was itching to drop Ten, and I wondered if that was a homophobic thing.

Asshole.

"They've put Bryan Delaney in goal," Jacob observed.

"Yeah, I saw. He did okay last time."

"He doesn't look so good, though."

I apparently missed something as I'd been staring at Jacob and not the screen. In fact, I'd take every opportunity to stare at him.

I have this bad.

"Where?" I asked and paused the feed. I skipped back to a point where the camera focused on Bryan and Ten talking. Ten was cupping Bryan's shoulder and seemed more serious than I had seen in a while, and even though Bryan was ready for the ice, he wasn't looking at Ten but past him at the other bench. Was there a story there?

"He'll be okay," I said, even though I had no idea if he would be. He was doing well for the Railers, and with people like Ten and Arvy on the team in front of him, the Railers were hungry for a win tonight.

We settled in for the game, and it started off fast and brutal. It seemed like the Raptors defensemen had one thing in mind, to take Ten out of the game. That was nothing unusual. Ten was too fast to get caught a lot of the time, and when he did get caught, he had this way of getting himself out of situations he didn't want to be in.

Adler Lockhart took offense at the fact that Petrov Egorov, a Raptor defenseman, got away with an uncalled slash on Lockhart. The cheers in the arena were impossibly loud, and I watched Adler do his best work.

"Way to go, Adler," Jacob said. "I love that man."

Every player partnered off with someone from the other

team, and Ten was right there, jumping into the mass of bodies, to pull one of the Raptors away.

Then everything got messy, skaters slipped and slid, and abruptly people separated, and there was silence. The cameras panned the audience, and everyone had quietened and were staring down at the ice.

What had happened?

The commentator was agitated. "It looks like we have a Railer down. The team's trainer is… is that Lockart… wait… it's Tennant Rowe. I can confirm that Tennant Rowe is on the ice. Is he moving? It doesn't look as if he's moving."

I stood, watching in horror as Bryan skated out of his crease and threw himself at Aarni Lankinen, slammed the man's face into the glass as the crowd around whoever was on the ice had faded back. Connor went straight over, the captain sliding to his knees, and there was blood. So much blood.

But it was obvious who was lying in the blood. Ten.

The replays showed Ten being pawed at in the melee, an accident causing his helmet to come off, and then the big Raptors defender launching himself at Ten, yanking Ten back over his skate and into the middle of the horde, right on his head.

They played it over and over again, from every conceivable angle, and nothing changed. There was still the awful pull, and the hit to the ice. All through this, the commentator was in shock and kept repeating the same words.

"Tennant Rowe isn't moving. This looks bad. The paramedics are with him."

Players were ordered back to the benches, but Connor stayed, along with Adler, both of them standing with bowed heads, talking to each other. Aarni was escorted off the ice.

There was so much blood. When the teams backed away, all I could see was Ten lying still, splayed on the ice like his strings had been cut.

"Tennant Rowe isn't moving. This looks bad. The paramedics are with him."

"... RYKER!"

Jacob's voice broke into my horror.

"Ten," I said and coughed to clear my throat. Oh God, what would Dad be going through? "Dad."

What did I do? I needed to go. I needed to go to the rink. I needed to see...I should go to... the hospital... was Ten alive... so much blood.

The door to my room flew open, Mom standing there, white as a sheet. "Ryker." She glanced from me to the television.

"I need to go to..."

"Ian will take you where you need to go, grab some stuff. He's getting the car out now."

I PICKED UP THE PHONE, looked Jacob in the eyes. He was blurred, but that was me. I was crying I think, and I felt sick. So fucking sick.

All I knew was that I had to get to Dad, needed to be there for him.

And for Ten.

Jacob was saying something. "Go with your stepdad, Ry, okay. Just go."

I ended the call, pocketed my cell, and glanced around. I was mostly still packed from getting there. So I grabbed what I could and left.

· · ·

THE ROOM WAS STILL. The only sound was that of machines beeping, and all I could see was my Dad's back. They'd let me in. I was family, and I'd gotten there before Ten's brothers, both of whom had games tonight, and a long time before his mom and dad, who lived some distance away.

This was my family, my Dad, his shoulders bent, alone in this room with Ten lying bandaged and quiet in bed.

"Dad?" I said quietly. I don't think he even knew I was in the room.

He turned to face me, agony carved into his face.

"A skate blade cut his neck," he said, his voice flat, emotionless. "He hasn't woken up yet. They stopped the bleeding. But he has…" Dad reached up and touched his temple. He looked broken, and I went a step closer, and then took another step until I had my Dad in my arms and held him tight.

"I'm here now," I kept repeating, my heart hurting, and my eyes wet. "Here for both of you."

SIXTEEN

Jacob

————

IT WAS ONE OF THE LEAST JOYOUS HOLIDAYS EVER. NOT ONLY was I burned out from exams and the stress of not knowing my grades yet, despite checking every miserable hour online, but I was also sick with worry for Tennant, Jared and Ryker. I spent every waking hour texting Ryker, hoping that constant communication would help him in some small way. We'd fallen asleep with each other a couple of times already, phones in hand. We were both miserable and scared. The news coming from the doctors was that Ten was probably done for the season, and that he was showing some brain issues.

Still, they said he was a fighter, that he was strong and young, and they were convinced he had every chance to get through this. They didn't put that in writing, hedged their responses to any questions, but overall everyone stayed positive.

I shuffled downstairs at the crack of dawn, eyes blurry and head muzzy but chore clothes on, to find my parents in the kitchen, sitting at the table with a small pile of presents. A jolt of concern shook me from my exhausted state.

"Sit down, son."

My father glanced at my chair. I sat in it. Mom got up, still in her robe and slippers, to get me a mug of coffee. No one said a word until I had my coffee cup in hand.

"Did someone die?" It was the first thing that came to mind. "Did you sell the farm?" That was the second.

"Jacob, do you love Ryker?" my father asked. No leading up to it or skirting around, just *wham!* right in the face like a wet sock.

I threw my mother a confused look. She gave me a tiny smile which eased the worry. A bit. "I uh… I think maybe I might. Why? Oh God, did something happen? Did Ten die?"

"No, Jacob, no." Mom reached across the scarred table to place her hand on my forearm. "No, we've not heard anything. Your father just, well, I'll let him talk."

My eyes flew back to Dad. He met my look. "You need to go be with Ryker during this trying time."

My brain sort of spun like a tractor in a muddy field. "But I'm needed here. Christmas… the milking…"

"We'll handle the chores. And as for Christmas, we'll miss you, but this year your boyfriend needs you more than we do. You can open your gifts now," Mom said, easing back into things, even though she'd said Dad would do the talking. Since he spoke very little, she usually had to fill in the gaping holes.

"If you love that boy, then your place is with him and his family." Dad pushed to his feet without taking his eyes from my face. "We'll manage. Go."

And he walked out, stopping only long enough to put his empty mug into the sink and give my neck a squeeze on the way past.

Mom and I sat there, frost thick on the windows, staring at each other. "Did he just tell me to go be with my boyfriend? I mean… is he cool with the gay now? I'm confused."

"He's a good man, Jacob. He's just slow to change. It's kind of a Benson thing."

"But is he cool with me? With my being—?"

"He's working on it. Now open your gifts and go pack. I wish we could afford to fly you to Harrisburg but…"

I left my chair to hug her tightly. "I promise I'll be home all summer to help. Maybe Ryker will be with me. Then you'll have two big galoots to feed."

She patted my back as we held each other. "We'll see what happens when summer comes. Now go shower and pack. It's a long drive to Harrisburg."

"I love you." I kissed her cheek, tore into my presents, kissed her yet again, and raced back to my room. Showering and packing took under an hour. Warming up my old Ford pickup took nearly half that long. When the truck was finally thawed, I paused long enough to glance at the milk barn. All the lights were lit. "I love you too, Dad."

Maybe someday I'd be man enough to tell him that to his face. Maybe someday I'd be man enough to tell Ryker as well. I hoped like hell those days would come soon.

THE DRIVE TOOK over eighteen hours. I didn't have any extra money to stop at a motel, so I drank cans of energy drinks bought at rest stops along the way, played lots of Keith Urban and Tim McGraw as loud as the speakers could take, and cracked the windows to keep the cab at about fifty degrees. Along the way, I picked up some gifts for my guy. Stupid shit, cheap shit, trinkets from gas stations that he'd probably throw away as soon as he could, but I wanted to have something to give him besides a hug and empty words.

I drove into the capital of Pennsylvania at one in the morning, my face cold from the wind blowing on it, a cup of fresh coffee —fresh to me not to the coffee itself—between my thighs, and a little something for Ryker's dinner, although dinnertime had long since passed. Gas station food. He'd probably get food poisoning from the chicken tenders and ranch dressing dip. Over our time together we'd learned a few things about each other. Things that we both liked and disliked. Ryker Madsen loved chicken tenders. He'd eat them for breakfast, lunch, dinner, and dessert. It was way beyond quirky, but it was a Ryker thing, and therefore I accepted it.

He'd talked about the rehab center Ten had been sent to, but it was late and I doubted he would be there now. I had his father's address because Mom had wanted to send them a Christmas card, so I fed it into Google Maps as Alan Jackson sang about having gone country. The big city surrounded me, making me feel as if I was about as far from having gone country as I had ever been. It must've been that I loved this man because the city and I didn't get along generally. Too many people in fancy suits, too many buildings, city slickers in my space and face. Give me rolling green fields, cows, the smell of freshly cut hay, pickup trucks, Wranglers, and brisk Minnesota air any time.

The driveway held three cars, Jared's, Ten's and one that I assumed was Ryker's. I recalled Ryker saying the press was hounding them steadily, trying to get into the hospital to snap images of Ten lying in bed or weeping family members hustling past. They'd also taken to showing up at Jared's place. Maybe Jared had installed a security system. Hell, maybe Stan had hired some Russian mafia goons to patrol the block. I threw a quick glance up and down the street, hoping I'd not see a dark sedan roll up to me. I wasn't sure how I'd handle four big Russians in suits bearing down on me. I guess

I could've whipped cold chicken tenders at them and then run away like the wind.

I didn't see anyone or anything that looked like a reporter or a Russian, so I exited my truck and padded quietly to the door, box of chicken tenders in one hand, my duffel bag in the other. I rang the bell a few times, feeling shitty about waking them at close to two in the morning.

"I swear to Christ, if one more of you assholes rings my fucking bell, I'm going to come unglued!"

When the door flew open and Jared glowered at me, I immediately coughed up an apology.

"I kind of came to see Ryker, but I can go back home if you need me to."

He gold-fished at me for a few moments. This his expression cleared.

"Don't be silly. He'll be glad to see you. Come in." Jared stumbled back from the door, his hair wrecked from tossing and turning by the looks of things, and his face drawn and wrinkled. He appeared much older than he had when I'd met him on campus. "He talks about you endlessly."

"Jacob?" We both turned to glance at Ryker standing just inside the living room. He looked as dreadful as Jared did. My heart broke into bits.

Jared sort of stepped into the shadows of the dimly lit room. I handed Ryker the cold chicken tenders. He opened the lid, blinked at the contents, and then grinned at me as if he'd found a vial of Wayne Gretzky's mojo in that Styrofoam container.

I couldn't take it any longer. I had to get him into my arms, so I grabbed him and hugged him, crushing the tenders between us. Ryker wiggled around, and then his mouth was on mine. We kissed for a long time, softly, just touching lips and whispering stupid stuff.

"Thanks for coming out. I just… it's been… everything is tough, and I'm fucking terrified of the future, and shit, it's good to have you here."

And those gruff words made the eighteen hours on the road all worth it. "Come on, let's warm up those tenders and talk."

We kissed more and talked and ate greasy chicken that gave us both killer heartburn. Then we crashed on his bed, sleeping until noon, his head tucked into my armpit, making me smile like an idiot when I woke up.

The next few days were hard. Ten was better, talking, smiling, walking, but he was slow, his speech broken and slurred, and his left side seemed weak, as if he'd had a stroke or something. There was specialty rehab, but I tried not to be too nosy when overhearing private matters. This wasn't my family. I was just kind of on the periphery as Ryker's support system.

Two days after my arrival, we had a small holiday thing in Tennant's hospital room. Just family, which I was humbled to be considered a part of. Even though the twenty-fifth was still a week away, everyone had decided to do this now, before Ten started rehab, so that he could focus on his recovery and not stress out over him not being able to get gifts for everyone, which he was, despite all his other massive concerns.

With me and Ryker and Mrs. Rowe all staying in the small two-bedroom apartment Jared had rented, things started to get tight, nerves began to fray, and worry began to weigh on every shoulder. Ten was not coming home. He was going for more rehab, and then they'd reevaluate him. Ten was ugly about this. Jared was beyond stressed. Mrs. Rowe baked. Ryker and I felt like we were underfoot and causing additional stress. The night we got the news about Ten and rehab, Ryker approached his father to ask if we could maybe head back to campus. There was nothing we could do here. The holiday—sad and low as it was—had been celebrated.

"And I think Ten doesn't need us here." Ryker piled on top of the reasons we'd listed. I stood in the corner of the kitchen, chewing on my bottom lip, feeling uneasy. "He just wants you, and we're getting in the way…"

"I understand." Jared sighed, rubbing at his tired eyes with the tips of his fingers. "We're all overloaded. Maybe it's time for me to go back to work as well. Give Ten the space he needs to recover without me hovering. He told me I hover. Took him a while, but he told me, and he was firm about it."

Ryker grabbed his father and held him tightly. Mrs. Rowe left the cookie dough on the pans to join in the hug. I tried to slip out of the kitchen, but Jared snaked out a hand and pulled me into the embrace. I may have teared up a bit.

"I'll call every day to check on Ten, I swear," Ryker vowed.

"I know, son. Now get moving, go see Ten, and then spend some time living your life. You've been a blessing to me during all of this." Jared kissed his son's thick hair. More tears may have been shed. After a shower and a long visit with Ten, Ryker and I began to pack for the trip back to campus. Classes would start in a few weeks, and now that Tennant was out of danger—we hoped—it was time to think about school again. Also, and this was total greed on my part, but if we went back early, the house I shared with the other Eagles would be all ours. Ryker couldn't get into his dorm, but we could get into the house. I had keys.

Ten days of alone and downtime, just me and him, was enticing to both of us. So, we said goodbye to Jared and Mrs. Rowe and set off to make the return trip to Minnesota. The drive back was so much more enjoyable. Ryker spelled me at the wheel. We ate hot dogs and chicken tenders from more gas stations, bickered over county music versus pop/rock/indie music, and tumbled deeper into love with each other with every mile clocked, or at least I was falling hard and fast. It was scary but thrilling.

But Ten was still foremost in both our minds. How easily life can change.

Morning was just breaking when we dragged our asses into the pit that was my home away from home. No one had cleaned up before leaving for the holiday break.

"Don't even look at it," Ryker said, taking me by the arm and pulling me to the stairs. "We'll clean it later. Come on, let's go to bed. I'm tanked."

"Is that a used condom?"

"Jacob, no looking. Come on." He tugged strongly. I followed him up the stairs and into the room I shared with Ben. Thankfully, it was super tidy. "There, see, clean and neat. Now you can wipe that disgusted look off your face."

He pulled his shirt over his head. The revolted expression melted away. God, he was beautiful. Tall and strong, firm, muscled. Ryker was tightly made masculine perfection, a flawless example of athletic beauty. We'd been apart for weeks. I had to touch him, just for a minute, and then we could grab some desperately needed sleep. He was busy pushing the twin beds together and so never saw me coming up behind him. He jumped in fright when I wrapped my arms around his middle, the shout a bit high for such a buff guy.

We wrestled around for a minute, him upset with me scaring him. The playful jostling turned into heated stroking, his mouth pliant when I stole a kiss. Sleep, which I'd wanted more than anything forty minutes ago, had become a forgotten concern. Now, all I wanted was Ryker. We ripped our clothes as we lapped and licked each other's mouths. He hooked his leg around mine and twisted us up, knocking me off-balance. We fell across the beds, naked, rigid cocks grinding into each other's hips or legs. It was a divine madness. Ryker pulled away, his thigh between mine, and gyrated into me, his prick hard and slick from precum. I roughly rolled him to his back, grabbing his arms and holding them over his head.

I claimed his mouth with a kiss that left him squirmy and needy under me. When I let go of his wrists, he wrangled me to my back, his hair hanging into his face as he rolled his hips in a slow circle, his cock bumping mine with each heated movement. My body was on fire, my skin hot as lava, and I wanted him so badly I was close to screaming in frustration. He played with my nipples and bit a path along my shoulder. I moved my leg, and he slipped between my thighs, his dick nudging at my ass as if he knew exactly what I wanted the most.

"Would you fuck me?" He stopped chewing on my neck and looked down at me blankly. I reached up to push the hair from his sticky cheeks. "I've been waiting for someone special. Someone I cared about, someone I loved."

"And that's me?" His voice was weak and wobbly, my playful, sexy Ryker now gone. A kind of stupefied Ryker had taken his place.

"Yeah, dummy, that's you." He lowered himself, his mouth settling on mine, his tongue gently slipping into my mouth as I lifted my hips from the bed, hoping to encourage him even more. The kiss went on and on, our lips slick and tender when we broke apart. "Will you fuck me?"

"No," he replied in a breathy sort of exhalation that made my eyes widen. "I'll make love to you because… because I love you too."

Hearing those words made me harder and softer all at

once. My body was primed for sex now, my heart tender and open to him. God, but I wanted him inside me. Both of us were shaky with need and we applied gallons of lube to his cock. Seriously, thick droplets of lube dribbled to the sheets. We both sniggered at that, our smiles slowly slipping away when he climbed back between my legs.

"I think you need to hold onto your legs," he said, pressing my knees into my chest.

I grabbed my legs and hugged them, anxious and aroused, my eyes on his prick until I couldn't see it anymore. I felt him though, the round head of his cock, pressing gently on my hole, as he steadied himself on his knees, one hand on my leg, the other firmly gripping his cock. I looked up from his smooth chest to his face and fell into his eyes. "Say stop anytime. I love you."

"I love you too, and it'll be fine." He thrust. I yelped in shock and pain, and he immediately pulled out, concern thick on his face.

"No! Slow down, shit. Fuck. Get more lube."

"More lube?" He sounded kind of incredulous.

I nodded, and he did as asked and tried again. I came to realize that we could have been wallowing in a lake of lubrication and the sensations would have been the same. The burn and stretch as he eased into me, pushing deeper and deeper, made me wince and groan. I stopped him several times, a hand to his chest or grabbing at his side until all of him was deep inside me. "How is it?"

He was shaky, kind of pale, but hot… so incredibly hot. His pupils were huge, his cheeks damp with sweat, and his lips soft and in need of kissing. Shame I couldn't reach them.

"Good," I huffed, trying to find the pleasure in this possession. He moved a bit, rolling his hips, and I gasped.

"Oh… okay yeah, that's nice." He did it again, and I groaned. "You like it? Do I feel good?"

"You feel fucking amazing," he replied gruffly, his fingers roaming down the inside of my thighs to take my cock and balls in hand. "Hot and tight, slick. Does it hurt?"

"At first, but now…" Now I wasn't sure. It was a sweet kind of pain that I couldn't quite describe. "Now it's mostly okay."

He nodded, stroking my cock and fondling my balls as I held myself open for him.

"Move now, easy, easy, not fast. Yeah, good, better. Shit, oh man, Ryker, that's—yeah, slow. Don't pound me, okay, please."

"I won't, I promise. Damn you're so tight." He eased out an inch, then pushed back in. "I really want to come. Shit, I need to come now."

He went deep, leaning into me with all his weight. My eyes closed. The depth made me grimace and moan, not sure if I wanted him out of me now or if I wanted him buried inside me like this forever. I felt his cock kicking, and I came in his hand, coating his fingers with spunk.

"Oh hell," he gasped, rocking up higher on his knees to get even deeper. "I can feel your ass pulling on me. Fuck, fuck. Ah shit, Jacob, I fucking love this."

I grunted something in reply, my body too bound up in my release to speak intelligently. He eased out of me once the trembling subsided. I released my legs slowly, fearing cramps, and lay there across mine and Ben's beds, trying to sort out my first time bottoming.

"You look like someone just crammed a grenade up your ass," Ryker said.

"Kind of feels like that."

"You hated it." He sighed, falling back into bed after

attending to the condom. "I could tell you hated it. You should have stopped me."

"No, I didn't hate it. I just... it wasn't—it just wasn't quite what I expected,." I flopped to my side so I could see him. He was staring at the ceiling, his face puckered, his hair sticking to his face as his chest rose and fell rapidly. "You did great." I pushed up to rest on an elbow, my fingers tracing his beautiful pouty bottom lip. "Super considerate, sweet, gentle."

"But you hated it." He squeezed his eyes tightly shut. "I wanted you to like it."

"I did like it. I came like a rhino, didn't I?"

"I guess, yeah."

"You were so good. I loved how slow you went." I bent over to kiss him. He rolled into me, greedy for my kisses and probably for some easing of his guilt over hurting me. I'd kind of expected a little pain, so he didn't need to feel remorse over it. "Next time it'll be better."

"You *want* a next time?" He pushed me to my back, straddling me, his eyes bright now. "I mean, be totally honest, okay? If you don't like anal, I get that because like, hello? I couldn't deal with a finger in my ass too well at first."

My head felt heavy as it rested on his pillow. Actually, my whole being was sated and calm, my muscles loosening up.

"I totally want a next time." My ass twitched. "Just not for a day or two."

He settled on me, chest to chest, and lapped into my mouth. "I love that you're such a big old Nellie bottom."

"Fuck you, Madsen." I chuckled, then pinned him to the bed and made him come in record time with just one finger working his prostate and some really filthy words. When he was a quivering ball of incoherent noises, I licked the last pearly droplet of cum from the head of his prick, then patted his heaving, sperm-speckled chest soundly, smearing his spend into the thin trail of dark hair trailing down his belly. "Imagine what I could do with three fingers and my mouth."

He shuddered violently. "That'll be *my* next time."

Okay, so now *that* there was a challenge this big old Nellie bottom was going to make sure to take him up on. Tomorrow.

Epilogue

RYKER

THE NEXT DAY I CALLED DAD. HE STILL LOOKED TIRED.

"Are you still not sleeping, Dad?" I asked him when we FaceTimed that morning.

"I am. Don't worry about me."

I huffed because Dad was so damn stoic, and it was grating on my last nerve. Who else would worry about him? The team? Yeah, I'm sure they were all there for him, but I was his son, and it was my job to look out for him.

"I do worry. You look too tired, and you should be sleeping because Ten isn't there."

I knew as soon as I said this that, I was wrong. I'd gotten used to sleeping with Jacob, and the thought of not having him close by for any length of time was hard.

Dad pinched the bridge of his nose. "When I close my eyes…"

I see Ten. The blood, the pain. I want to stop it, but I can't, and I'm terrified.

"I love you, Dad," I blurted.

He smiled then, but it was a shaky smile. "Ten got you a present before…" the accident was left unsaid.

"I'm visiting for New Year's, and you can both watch when I open his gift then. Is it ridiculously expensive and will it end up turning me into a spoiled brat?"

Dad laughed, and it sounded warm and spontaneous. "You *are* a spoiled brat."

I thought about Jacob and how he saw me, and I knew without a doubt I was anything but that now.

"And whose fault is that?" I teased. "How is Ten getting along now?"

Dad smiled, and it seemed completely natural. "The doctors are actually saying he could be back on his skates. That his healing is going faster than they imagined."

"This season?"

"I don't think so Ry, but Ten is special. I have hope. We should all have hope."

"I love you, Dad."

"Love you too, son."

We ended the call, and I was feeling kind of melancholy, wishing that Jacob would hurry home already. I'd been sitting in the front room of the shared house for a while now, waiting on him.

The door opened, and a tree walked in. Or rather Jacob walked in with a sickly-looking pine, that had to be the last in some back-street lot.

"I couldn't leave it." He placed it down in the corner and fought to prop it up with the chair. At last, it stayed, and by that time, I was up and at his side.

"This was the runt of the litter, wasn't it?" I poked at it and felt immediate guilt when it shed on me.

Jacob jabbed my arm. "Leave the poor thing alone."

"What do you plan on doing with it?"

He sighed heavily and shrugged. "I thought that, together, we could make it beautiful."

That was Jacob, so pragmatic and independent and focused on the land and his hopes for the farm, and then in the next moment picking up some abandoned tree he'd found so we could make it beautiful.

I tugged him to face me, cradled his face, and kissed him gently. This man was all mine and was joining me at Dad's for New Year's. The reason being something to do with cows and family and his own dad, although he mumbled most of it last night in bed.

He'd passed all his exams, and ultimately when he graduated and I went off to Arizona, we'd have to work damn hard to stay together. I guess that was a bridge we'd have to cross when we got there.

"I love you," he said, and kissed me again, this time turning me around so I was pressed half against the tree and half against the wall.

When we made love, it was slow and sweet, and I told him I loved him so many times.

It was just a shame about the prickles from the tree because those suckers got everywhere.

THE END

Scott (Owatonna U, 2)

What happens when you try to fix the past and end up threatening your future?

Scott

Scott is struggling. Grieving the loss of his brother, carrying the weight of his father's expectations, and getting his ass kicked in the rink. He's in a downward spiral. He needs a solution and fast, but when his steroid use is exposed, he's close to losing his place at Owatonna and more importantly, on the Eagles Hockey team. Thrown out of his house, with nowhere to go and no future in sight, he only has one choice; agree to mandatory counseling, random drug tests, and get his act together. Only then will he have a chance at normal. Meeting Hayne, a senior connected to the world through his art, is a shock to the system. Moving in with him is his only option, but falling for the shy artist leaves Scott in an impossible situation, and one he can't escape.

Hayne has always been that quiet, creative kid who sat in the back of the class drawing instead of listening to the teacher. A talented artist, the shy and sensitive young man is struggling with the loss of his childhood friend. Seeing his sadness reflected in his usually colorful paintings, he decides to attend grief counseling and meets Scott, a lost soul in desperate need of light and color in his life. Taking in a homeless hockey player certainly was never part of his carefully orchestrated ten-year plan. But now that Scott is in his life, he's discovering the joy of this man's loving smile and tender touch is one of the most beautiful palettes on earth.

Hockey Series' from RJ Scott & V.L. Locey

Harrisburg Railers

Owatonna U Hockey

Arizona Raptors

Boston Rebels

LA Storm

Chesterford Coyotes - Young Adult

When hockey wunderkind Tennant Rowe meets his new coach, he knows he's in trouble. Jared Madsen is nine years older than Tennant, impossibly attractive, and — worst of all — his brother's off-limits best friend. Is their chemistry worth the risk?

Changing Lines (Railers 1)

Can Tennant show Jared that age is just a number, and that love is all that matters?

The Rowe Brothers are famous hockey hotshots, but as the youngest of the trio, Tennant has always had to play against his brothers' reputations. To get out of their shadows, and against their advice, he accepts a trade to the Harrisburg Railers, where he runs into Jared Madsen. Mads is an old family friend and his brother's one-time teammate. Mads is Tennant's new coach. And Mads is the sexiest thing he's ever laid eyes on.

Jared Madsen's hockey career was cut short by a fault in his heart, but coaching keeps him close to the game. When Ten is traded to the team, his carefully organized world is thrown into chaos. Nine years his junior and his best friend's brother, he knows Ten is strictly off-limits, but as soon as he sees Ten's moves, on and off the ice, he knows that his heart could get him into trouble again.

Changing Lines

Harrisburg Railers (Hockey Romance)

1. Changing Lines
2. First Season
3. Deep Edge
4. Poke Check
5. Last Defense
6. Goal Line
7. Neutral Zone
8. Hat Trick
9. Save The Date
10. Baby Makes Three
11. Rivals
12. Perfect Gifts
13. Family First

Railers Volume 1 | Railers Volume 2 | Railers Volume 3 | Railers Volume 4

Coast to Coast (Arizona Raptors 1)

Coast To Coast

When opposites attract, this bottom-of-the-league team will never be the same again.

A stipulation in his father's will forces Mark back into the arms of a family that disowned him and leaves him one-third owner of a hockey team facing financial ruin. He doesn't even watch hockey, let alone like it, and wants nothing more than to head back to New York. Then there's the new coach, a stubborn, opinionated, irritating man with superiority issues and questionable music taste. Butting heads with Rowen becomes the new normal, but it comes with passionate debate and an all-consuming lust.

Challenged to rebuild one of the worst teams in the league into a future cup contender, Rowen can't pass up the opportunity. Never in his twenty years of hockey has he ever seen a team managed so badly or coached players overflowing with resentment and bigotry. Yet there's something about this team and this city that compels him to roll up his sleeves and start dismantling. If only Mark, one of three siblings who now own the Raptors, wasn't so damned rock-headed yet so damned appealing his job might be easier. It doesn't look like either is willing to give in, but one night in a dark, desert hotel changes everything.

Coast To Coast

Arizona Raptors (Hockey Romance)

1. Coast To Coast
2. Across the Pond
3. Shadow and Light
4. Sugar and Ice
5. School and Rock

Top Shelf (Boston Rebels 1)

Top Shelf

Acting on the attraction to his best friend's brother has always been off the table for Xander until a passionate hookup with Mason at a beach resort begins a love affair that burns long after summer ends.

Mason specializes in assisting same-sex couples on their journey to becoming parents and fighting every rule that blocks his way in the stuck-in-the-past agency that hired him. Living in his brother's pool house is rent-free, and every cent he earns he saves for his dream—that one day he'd have his own company helping others. The downside is that he has to see his annoying brother every day, the upside is that his brother's teammates from the Boston Rebels make regular visits. The eye candy that passes Mason's window is almost enough to make him consider dating a hockey player, but not just any player though. Ever since Xander—his brother's childhood friend—came out as gay at a press conference, Mason's puppy love has turned into a burning attraction he can no longer ignore.

Hockey has been one of Xander's main focuses since he was old enough to balance on skates. Well, hockey and Mason Kingsley, but Mason was always unattainable. Now that he's about to see thirty candles on his birthday cake and is no longer hiding the fact he's gay, he's ready to find a soul mate to make his life complete. A summer vacation is just what he needs to have time to think, but when the Boston Rebels arriving in paradise with Mason in tow, thinking is the last thing he needs. One torrid night under a balmy moon and rules about not messing with his best friend's brother vanish on a warm, tropical breeze.

Summer romances don't generally last past Labor Day, but with the new season about to begin Xander and Mason are going to have to face the world and decide if their love is real enough to withstand everything.

Top Shelf

Boston Rebels

Lost In Boston (Free Prequel Novella)

1. Top Shelf
2. Back Check
3. Snowed
4. Royal Lines
5. Blade

6. Rental

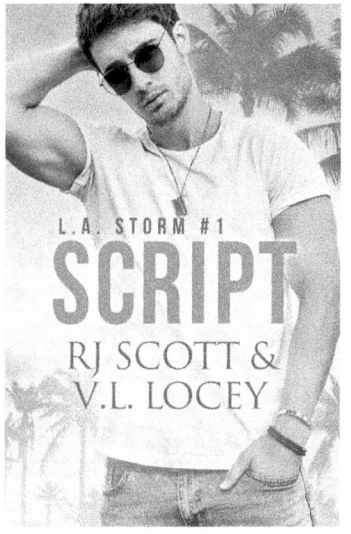

Script (LA Storm, 1)

Script

**Hollywood A-lister Finn might be Canadian, but he needs
Cameron to show him how to hockey.**

Actor Finn Kerrigan is at a crossroads. After growing up a soap star,
then starring in a hugely successful trilogy of action movies, he's
finally given the chance to read a heartfelt and passionate script that
could change his life forever. The role would be enough for people
to see him as a serious actor, and maybe even win him an award or
two (and no, a golden raspberry award for his action movies doesn't
count). Once established as a serious actor he's sure he can come out

of the closet and finally live his truth. When he lies to get the part of a hockey player on a struggling team, he suddenly has nowhere to hide. He might be Canadian, but the last time he skated he was ten, and no, he doesn't have hockey in his blood. With only a month until filming starts, he about to be exposed, but partnered with a player who's supposed to be giving him tips, he doesn't realize how many of his secrets will come to light. Falling in lust, one heated kiss at a time, is inevitable, but giving Cameron up at the end of the shoot could break his heart.

Cameron Chavkin is the face of the LA Storm. And the body, and the hair, and the smile. He's at the prime of his career, men and women want to be with him, and he's skating better than he ever has before. His house sits next to a famous rock star's mansion, his garage is filled with expensive cars, and he's even been asked to mentor a once-famous actor in a new hockey movie. Life is pretty sweet. Until the bad boy of hockey meets Finn, a man on the edge with more secrets than Cameron has endorsements. Knowing better than to get involved, Cameron is swept up despite himself, and when it's time to say goodbye to the Storm's most eligible bachelor is finding it hard to follow the script.

Script

LA Storm

Chesterford Coyotes, Young Adult
Romance

Off The Ice (Chesterford Coyotes, 1)

Off The Ice

**A coming-of-age love story with high school, hockey rivalry,
friendship, family, and coming out.**

Soren's life changes in an instant when he and his younger brother
are adopted by hockey royalty. Making sense of his new life is hard
enough, but when he's enrolled in a private school it means facing a
whole new set of problems. Navigating friendship, family, and
hockey is one thing, but being attracted to the boy who vexes him is
a whole new thing.

Felix has a reputation to protect. He's the kid who seems to have everything but looks can be deceiving. Spinning lies about his perfect life, he's created a fantasy world that even he has started to believe. Only, it's not long before everything crumbles, all of his pretty lies are revealed, and only his closest rival sees through his pain and stands by him.

Fighting is easy, friendship is hard, but love is everything.

Off The Ice

Chesterford Coyotes

1. Off The Ice
2. On Thin Ice
3. *Dance on Ice*

Also By RJ Scott

For a full list of ebooks and links please scan the code above or visit
rjscott.co.uk/rjbooks

Meet RJ Scott

RJ discovered romance in books at a very young age and realized that if there wasn't romance on the page, she could create it in her head. With over one hundred and fifty books published, she is a full time author of gay romance.

She lives and works out of her home in the beautiful English countryside, spends her spare time reading, watching films, and enjoying time with her family.

The last time she had a week's break from writing she didn't like it one little bit and has yet to meet a box of chocolates she couldn't defeat.

www.rjscott.co.uk | rj@rjscott.co.uk

NEWSLETTER - rjscott.co.uk/rjnews

facebook.com/author.rjscott

x.com/Rjscott_author

instagram.com/rjscott_author

amazon.com/author/rj-scott

bookbub.com/authors/rj-scott

goodreads.com/rjscott

pinterest.com/rjscottauthor

Also By VL Locey

For a full list of ebooks and links please scan the code above or visit
vllocey.com/stories-from-vl-locey

Meet V.L. Locey

V.L. Locey loves worn jeans, yoga, belly laughs, walking, reading and writing lusty tales, Greek mythology, the New York Rangers, comic books, and coffee.

(Not necessarily in that order.)

She shares her life with her husband, her daughter, one dog, two cats, a flock of assorted domestic fowl, and two Jersey steers.

When not writing spicy romances, she enjoys spending her day with her menagerie in the rolling hills of Pennsylvania with a cup of fresh java in hand.

vllocey.com
vicki@vllocey.com

Newsletter - vllocey.com/newsletter

facebook.com/V.L.Locey
x.com/vllocey
instagram.com/vl_locey
bookbub.com/authors/v-l-locey
goodreads.com/vllocey
pinterest.com/vllocey